Here is a list of things
people have said about Nina Soni.

"Nina Soni is many things: Indian American, a list-maker, a word-definer, and a big sister. She is funny, observant, and smart, and she can also sometimes be a bit forgetful. The number one thing that Nina is? Loveable! I adore Nina and know readers will, too."
—Debbi Michiko Florence, author of
the Jasmine Toguchi series

"A perfect fit for readers who enjoy realistic fiction about friendship and self-discovery."
—*School Library Journal*

"…a flawed but refreshing and very likable protagonist…"
—*Booklist*

"A sweet and entertaining series opener about family and friendship."
—*Kirkus Reviews*

She's a phenomenon!

Phe-no-me-non means a happening or an event.

To all my grandchildren and to all those who have
welcomed my family and me into their homes

—K. S.

Published by
PEACHTREE PUBLISHING COMPANY INC.
1700 Chattahoochee Avenue
Atlanta, Georgia 30318-2112
*PeachtreeBooks.com*

Text © 2023 by Kashmira Sheth
Illustrations © 2023 by Jenn Kocsmiersky

Edited by Kathy Landwehr
Design and composition by Adela Pons
The illustrations were rendered digitally.

Printed and bound in February 2023 at Thomson Reuters, Eagan, MN, USA.
10 9 8 7 6 5 4 3 2 1 (hardcover)
10 9 8 7 6 5 4 3 2 1 (paperback)
First Edition
HC ISBN: 978-1-68263-501-8
PB ISBN: 978-1-68263-502-5

Cataloging-in-Publication Data is available from the Library of Congress.

# NINA SONI

## PERFECT HOSTESS

Written by **Kashmira Sheth**
Illustrated by **Jenn Kocsmiersky**

PEACHTREE
ATLANTA

**CHAPTER ONE**

I rushed out of my class as soon as school was done. My sister Kavita was supposed to be waiting for me by the front door of the building. She wasn't there.

I was about to go to her classroom when she peeked around the corner. "Nina!"

"There you are. I was terrified," I said. Even though I wasn't at all. But I would have been if she had stayed hidden.

Ter-ri-fied means you're so scared you almost forget to breathe.

When we stepped outside, the wind blew my hair. "Please zip up your jacket, Kavita," I said. It was the end of April, but it was still pretty cold.

I scanned the playground, wondering where my best friend Jay was. Most days, Kavita and I walk home with him because he lives on our street.

Kavita tugged at my sleeve. "Are you looking for that corner?"

Kavita is in first grade and asks me lots of questions. She thinks I have all the answers because I'm in fourth grade. The problem is, sometimes I don't even understand her questions. Like right now.

Jay came up behind us. He must have heard Kavita because he asked, "Which corner?"

"The corner where spring is," Kavita replied.

Jay's green eyes filled with confusion.

"Never mind," I said.

"Oh, we should mind," Kavita said. "If we don't, we won't have spring."

"That is totally, totally—" Jay looked at me. "Nina?"

"Absurd?" I suggested. Maybe that was the word he was looking for.

Kavita tugged at my mitten, and it came off. "What does 'absurd' mean?"

I pulled my mitten back on. "'Absurd' means something super-silly."

"No!" Kavita's cheeks puffed up. "What Mrs. Jabs said is not super-silly."

"Whoa." Jay put up his palm like he was telling us to stop. "What does your teacher have to do with spring and corners?"

"Mrs. Jabs said that spring is around the corner. And I don't know where that corner is. Do you, Jay?"

"Now I get it," he said.

I finally understood what Kavita was talking about too.

"Sometimes"—Kavita tapped his shoulder—"you are slow to catch on, Jay. But you do get things in the end."

"Thanks," he said. "I've always wanted that compliment."

"You did?" Kavita glanced at me. "Nina, does he really mean that? Or is he being sar-cas-tic?"

Kavita had broken the word "sarcastic" into separate syllables, like she wasn't sure she was saying it right. I gave her a mittened high five. "Hey, you remembered! It's because I used it before, right?"

"I had forgotten how to say it, but then I asked Dad."

"And now you know," I said.

Jay gave me a thumbs-up behind her back. "Kavita," he said as we turned onto our street, "the corner you're waiting for is in three days. It's going to be warm and sunny by Saturday. Then it will be spring."

"Yay, spring is almost here!" Kavita ran to our house.

"You made Kavita happy, Jay," I said. "Thanks."

"No problem." Jay walked toward his house. "See you tomorrow."

"Yup."

I followed Kavita into ours. As soon as I got inside, I

heard Kavita ask Mom, "Did you know that spring is just around the Saturday corner?"

"Thanks for telling me." Mom hugged us both. "Now I do."

"Maybe we can plant some flowers this weekend?" I asked. Mom loves gardening, so I was sure she would say yes.

"If we have time. We have guests coming."

Kavita clapped. "You mean we have guests who are coming 'round the corner? You know, like in the song, 'she'll be coming 'round the mountain when she comes'?"

Mom smiled. "You could say that."

"Who's coming? Is it Priya and her family?" I asked.

Priya is my friend, and her brother Nayan is Kavita's friend. And her parents are Mom and Dad's old friends. They live only an hour away and we often visit each other.

"No." Mom pointed to the kitchen. "While you have your snack, I'll tell you all about our guests."

I was so anxious to find out that I spilled the milk I was pouring for Kavita.

"Be careful," Mom said.

I grabbed a paper towel and cleaned up the mess before I sat at the table. I picked up a slice of zucchini bread. It was soft, and I was afraid it would crumble in my hand, so I shoved it into my mouth. The whole piece. It was bigger than my mouth, but I found that out too late. I had to keep my mouth closed and keep on chewing. I must have looked like my stuffed animal Lucky, who is a beaver.

Mom said, "Dadi and Montu are coming."

I was so excited that I felt my eyes grow as big as my mouth. Dadi is my grandmother and Montu is my cousin. Montu's younger than me, but older than Kavita. That means he is in the middle of us. They live in India, and this would be their first trip to the United States.

I covered my mouth with my hand and finished chewing. "Yay! Dadi and Montu are coming!" Mom didn't seem to hear me. I think the words got chewed up along with the zucchini bread.

*"They'll be coming 'round the corner when they come. They'll be coming 'round the corner when they come,"* Kavita

sang. She had not stuffed her mouth, so she could not only talk, but also sing.

As soon as I finished chewing, I took three gulps of milk right in a row. Then I wiped my mouth with a napkin. Now I could speak clearly. "When are they coming, Mom?"

"In three days."

"They'll bring spring with them!" Kavita said.

"You mean on Saturday?" I couldn't believe it. "Did you just find that out, or were you keeping it a secret from us?"

"Remember, last year they had to cancel their trip and we were all disappointed?" Mom said. "This time, your dad and I waited until we were sure they were coming to mention it."

They weren't supposed to arrive until Saturday, so I knew something could still go wrong and they could have to cancel their trip. "Mom, are you certain they'll come this time?" I asked.

"Yes." She smoothed my hair. "They called this morning after you went to school. They have packed their suitcases and are almost ready to hop on a plane."

"But they won't arrive for three days?" I was confused.

"Remember, it's a long journey, so you have to think about the travel time. Also, India is ten-and-a-half hours ahead of us. What time is it in India?"

"Let me calculate," I said. I did the math in my head.

It was 3:30 p.m. here.

If our time zones were 12 hours apart it would be 3:30 a.m. in India.

But Dadi and Montu are 10-1/2 hours ahead of us, which is 1-1/2 hours less than 12 hours, so I subtracted 1-1/2 hours from 3:30 a.m.

3:30 − 1:30 = 2:00

"It's two o'clock on Thursday morning there," I said. "They should be fast asleep."

"Right," Mom said. "They also have two nine-hour flights plus a layover of six hours in Europe."

I added it all up.

9 + 9 + 6 = 24

24 hours = 1 day

"That's a whole day!"

"Correct." Mom patted my back. "You solved that math problem quite quickly."

Kavita asked, "Do they have to get to the airport early, like we do?"

"Good thinking, Kavita," I said. "It's an international flight, so they probably have to get there at least three hours before the plane takes off, right, Mom?"

"Yes."

"That means they must be almost ready to fly." I took a sip of milk. "Mom, I'm so happy they're coming!"

Kavita raised her hand. "Me too."

"What do we need to do before Dadi and Montu arrive?" I got up from my chair. "I can help."

Kavita started singing again. *We'll be having so much fun when they come. We'll be having so much fun when they come.*

"Well." Mom pointed at a couple of bites of food on Kavita's plate and some milk in my glass. "Sit down and finish your snack, get your homework done, and then we will talk about all the things we need to do."

## CHAPTER TWO

Since I had worked out Dadi and Montu's travel time, my brain was prepared for my math homework. I solved all the problems I'd been assigned while Mom and Kavita went over some papers that Mrs. Jabs had sent home.

As soon as I was done, I asked, "Can I make a list of the things we need to do, Mom?"

"That would be wonderful," she replied.

My brain has too many train tracks—I mean *idea* tracks. Sometimes that makes it hard to deal with all of my ideas. That's why I love lists. They help me keep everything in my brain neat because they're straight up and down and not like sprinkles scattered all over a doughnut. I have a notebook called Sakhi where I write down my lists.

Sakhi means friend in Hindi.

Kavita and I know some Hindi because our parents speak it.

I went up to my bedroom. It looked clean. Mom must have already vacuumed and dusted. I picked up Sakhi from my desk and brought it downstairs.

Kavita was waiting at the table with paper and crayons.

"What are you going to draw?" I asked.

"Our new family," she replied.

"We don't have a new family."

"We will soon." She picked up a bright orange crayon. "We have our old family—that's four people—plus two new people, Dadi and Montu." She counted on her fingers.

"That means we'll have six people. That makes our old family a new family."

"I see," I said, even though I didn't think having family members come visit meant our family would be "new."

I opened Sakhi and wrote.

Things to do before Dadi and Montu arrive

* Clean up the house (Mom and Dad always do that before we have any guests. Dadi and Montu would be special guests, so we needed our house extra-clean).
* Get the guest bedroom ready.
* Buy healthy groceries for six people.
* Make a list of treats we should get for them (and us, because they wouldn't want to eat ice cream and pastries alone).
* Make a welcome sign.
* Make a list of activities we can do with them.

Now I had two more lists to make—one for treats and one for activities. Yay!

I glanced out the window. Not only was spring coming around the corner, it was bringing guests with it too! I wanted to be a very good hostess for Dadi and Montu. I wanted to be perfect.

"Perfect" sounded so mature.

> **Ma-ture** means all grown-up and behaving properly.

I made a list of how a mature perfect hostess would be and what she would do.

* She is always kind.
* She makes her guests feel welcome.
* She makes sure they're comfortable.
* She is patient when she teaches them something they don't know.
* She doesn't fight with them.

This list would help me become Nina Soni, Perfect Hostess.

"How many days will Dadi and Montu stay with us?" I asked.

Mom put the chopped cauliflower in a colander and washed it. "Six weeks."

"What?" Sakhi slipped from my hand and fell to the floor. I picked up my notebook. I was confused. "Can Montu miss that much school?"

Mom put oil in a pan to heat and added mustard seeds. "Montu is on summer break from now until the second week of June."

"When Montu is here, we will still have to go to school." Kavita put her hands on her hips. "Not fair."

The mustard seeds started popping. Mom dropped the cauliflower in the pan. It sizzled. "Fair or not, that's how it's going to be. You can stay home when you have your summer break."

"But it's not—"

Mom held up the spatula. "End of discussion."

When she says these three words, we know the rule. It means no more arguments or whining.

Now Kavita was grumpy, and Mom was not in that great a mood either.

It was my chance to be the mature older sister. "Montu might sleep in late because of the time difference," I said to Kavita. "He'll be ready to play with us when we get home."

"But then I'll be tired."

"Don't you play, dance, and sing after school? You even make up songs. You're never tired after school even though it takes a lot of energy to be creative."

"What does that mean?"

I explained, "'Creative' means when you make something new. Like songs or drawings."

"Yay!" She sang, *"I'll be bouncy, flouncy, trouncy to play with Montu when I get home."*

"And spend time with Dadi. Don't forget that she's coming too." I glanced at Mom. She gave me a happy smile.

"Kavita, will you help me make a list of treats we should buy for our guests?" I asked.

Her eyes sparkled as she nodded.

Treats for our guests

* Ice cream
* Chocolate
* Raisins, figs, and dates (healthy treats)
* Fried lentil chips (an Indian treat)
* Corn chips, salsa, avocados, and black beans for nachos
* Cookies
* Almonds, walnuts, and peanuts
* Cheese (many different kinds because they are yummy)

"They may want to go to the store and pick out something for themselves," Mom suggested.

I put one more thing down.

"Mom, what do you think Dadi and Montu would like to do?" I asked.

Kavita sang, *"Eat, drink and play, play, play. Sleep and rest and play again."*

I flipped a page and started the next list.

Things to do with Dadi and Montu

✳ Play (I didn't write "eat," "drink," "sleep," or "rest." I mean, those are necessary).

✳ Show them around Madison.

✳ Share new foods like pizza, macaroni and cheese, and enchiladas.

✳ Learn to read and write Hindi (from Dadi).

✳ Help Dadi cook.

✳ Go for walks.

✳ Share books and toys with Montu.

"Let's go down Nina's list and start tackling the chores," Mom said.

I checked my list in Sakhi. "The first is to clean the house."

"I already cleaned the upstairs and the basement and bought the groceries," Mom said.

I looked around. "The kitchen is not dirty."

"If you can pick up your stuff from the family room, I'll wipe the kitchen cupboards and appliances and mop the floor," Mom said.

"Let's do it."

When we were finished, I said, "The next thing is to get Dadi and Montu's beds ready."

"I can't make beds on my own," Kavita said. "But I love helping Dad make them."

"Let's go downstairs and make them together," I said. Our guest room is in the basement. "I think Dadi would like the flower sheets. I can get them."

"We're not going to have Dadi and Montu sleep in the basement," Mom said. "They're coming from a warm climate, and our basement will feel too cold and damp."

"But Priya's parents sleep there when they visit us."

"Nina, they only stay for a night or two. Dadi and Montu will be here for a long time. Plus, I don't want Montu so close to the furnace room. They can sleep in our room." She pointed at the basement door. "Dad and I will move downstairs."

"But I won't be able to fall asleep if I know you're not nearby," Kavita said.

What would a perfect hostess do? I made a quick in-my-head list.

* Dadi and Montu were coming from thousands of miles away.
* They were going to stay with us for six weeks.
* Dadi is older. All of us should show her our respect.

❋ We needed to give them a proper bedroom.

❋ I have a brand-new trundle bed in my room. That's two beds in one. Dadi could sleep in the top one and Montu could pull out the other one for himself.

❋ It might be exciting to sleep downstairs all by myself.

❋ But it would be far away from everyone. And maybe it would be a little scary with the furnace and all kinds of other sounds.

❋ Maybe I could sleep in Kavita's room. She has a big bed, so we could share.

"What if Kavita and I share her room? Dadi and Montu can sleep in mine," I suggested.

"Six weeks is a long time," Mom said. "Are you sure you are up for that?"

It was my chance to be generous.

Gen-er-ous means happily giving things away. It could be money, clothes, or even a room.

"I want to do it," I said.

Mom hugged me. "That is so thoughtful of you."

Kavita folded her arms. "What about me? I'm giving half of my room to Nina, and no one even asked me."

You really can't give half a room, but I didn't say that. Instead, I asked, "Is it okay if I sleep in your room, Kavita?"

"Ninai," Kavita said, "you can sleep in my room whenever you want."

Kavita used to call me Ninai when she was little. Now she does it when she wants me to feel special. That gave me a warm, loving, and cozy feeling.

"It's very nice of you to share, Kavita." Mom turned off the stove. "Now that that's settled, we need to put our plan into action."

The three of us went up to Kavita's room.

Mom opened Kavita's closet. "Nina, I'll make enough room to hang your dresses and empty out the top half of Kavita's dresser for your other clothes. Could you please bring them in here?"

"What about the rest of my things?" I asked.

"If you bring all your stuff in here, there won't be any place for us to sleep," Kavita said.

"You're right." Mom turned to me. "Let's just transfer clothes, schoolbooks, and a few things."

"Okay." I went to my room. My laundry hamper was empty, so I put my clothes in it and carried it to Kavita's room. Mom arranged everything while I got Lucky, my hairbrush, hair bands, lip balm, and some other stuff.

Now most of my favorite things were no longer in my room, so even though it wasn't empty, it felt like someone else's room, not mine. That made me unsettled.

Un-set-tled means feeling like a lake on a windy day. Not calm and smooth.

*When Dadi and Montu stay in this room, it will be full again,* I thought.

"Nina," Mom called.

"Yes?" I brought my other things to my new room. Which really wasn't mine or new. Just new to me.

"What else is on your list?" Mom asked.

"Make a welcome sign," I read.

Kavita pulled my arm. "Can we do it together, Nina? Pleasie-please?"

"Sure. Why don't you bring your markers downstairs, and I'll get some paper? You can draw and I'll write."

"While you do that, I'll get the rest of our dinner ready," Mom said.

The phone rang just as we went downstairs. I answered. It was Jay.

"Hey," he said, "do you want to go to Grandpa Joe's cabin next weekend with us? Nora and Jeff will be there too. It will be super-fun."

Nora and Jeff are Jay's cousins. Jeff's my age and Nora is a couple years older than me. I turned to ask Mom and then remembered that Dadi and Montu were coming.

"Jay, I wish I could, but I can't," I said.

"Why not?"

"Because we're having special guests and they arrive

on Saturday. They're staying with us for six weeks." I pur-
posely didn't tell Jay who was coming to make him curious.

Cu-ri-ous mean you want to find out more about
something or someplace. Or even some people.

"Priya and her family are staying with you for that long?"

I laughed. "No, Dadi and Montu."

"Wow! From India? How long have you known that?
Why did you keep it a secret?"

Jay's questions came fast, and before I could answer
one, he fired another. "Does my mom know?"

His mom, Meera Masi, and my mom are friends, so she
might know. But I wasn't sure.

"Jay, I just found out today that they're coming. Really,
I did."

He was quiet.

"Jay?"

"I guess you won't be able to go to the cabin." He
sounded disappointed.

"Sorry."

"No worries," he said. "Bye."

"Bye," I said.

I was excited about Dadi's and Montu's visit, but it meant giving up my room for six weeks and it also meant that I couldn't go away with Jay. Even before Dadi and Montu arrived, I had already made two big sacrifices.

---

**Sac-ri-fice** means to give up something of yours for someone else.

---

Kavita was coloring away. I sat down at the dining table and wrote:

*Dadi and Montu,*

*Welcome!*

*We are so happy you're here.*

But it came out scribbly, wiggly, and confused. Just the way I felt.

"Your writing looks unhappy," Kavita said. "Can you make it look bright and cheerful to match my tulips and daffodils?"

She showed me her picture. It looked like a perfect spring welcome to me.

"That's nice. Maybe I'll make a new sign tomorrow," I said.

She shook her head. "We're running out of time."

"No, we have three more days." I pushed my chair back. "If you're in such a rush why don't you do it yourself?"

Kavita's eyes filled with sadness.

"Sorry," I said, and ran upstairs to my room.

I looked for Lucky and didn't find him. Then I realized he wasn't in there and that in a way, it wasn't "my room" anymore, at least for a while.

Could I go in Kavita's room to get Lucky? What if she came in and asked me to leave? She was sharing her room with me because I had asked her to. She was so nice about it. But I had been rude to her. Sometimes the way you speak can hurt like a slap or a kick. And now she might be angry with me. I decided to stay in my room. I had it for two more nights, so it was okay to sit on my bed.

I was only giving up my room for a few weeks. Still, I felt queasy.

> **Quea-sy** means you feel as if your stomach is getting squeezed. Like when you go for a sleepover and all of a sudden you start missing your family and home.

I made an in-my-head list about my feelings.

* I was happy that Dadi and Montu were coming.

* It had been my idea to give my room to them.

* Still, it wasn't going to be easy to do. Maybe I should have taken more time to think about whether I really wanted to do that.

* When I said no to going to the cabin with Jay, it made me sad.

* He was disappointed, and I felt bad.

* I made Kavita unhappy and again I felt bad.

* It is not easy to be a perfect hostess.

I sighed.

It was a lot of hard work to have guests, and Dadi and Montu had not even arrived yet.

## CHAPTER THREE

Mom woke Kavita and me early Saturday morning.

When we came downstairs, I poked my head out the front door. It was sunny and warm, and the air smelled fresh and light. Spring was here, just like Jay had said it would be. It was a perfect day to drive to Chicago to pick up Dadi and Montu from the O'Hare Airport.

"Where's Dad?" I asked Mom.

"He's in the garage getting the van ready. While you eat your breakfast, I'll shower."

Mom is a landscape architect, so we have a van because

she needs a big vehicle for all her stuff. Usually we don't use the third row of seats since there are only four of us. Mom and Dad sit in front, and Kavita and I sit in the middle row. Starting today, there would be six of us for a while, so Dad was putting the last row of seats back up.

Mom had already set out two bowls of cereal and the carton of milk on the kitchen table. I picked up an almond from my bowl and ate it. "Kavita, on our way home, you'll have to sit all the way in the back because Mom or Dadi will sit in your place."

She was quiet at first. But Kavita talks or sings all the time, so I didn't have to wait very long for her to respond. "Where will you sit, Nina?"

I poured milk in each of our bowls. "I'm older than Montu, so I get to keep my seat."

"But he is our guest. Guests first!"

Now I was lost. In a way Kavita was right. If Montu was our guest, maybe I should give him my place. But weren't he and Dadi our family? So did I have to let him sit in my seat?

Wherever I sat on the first day would probably be my place for their entire visit. That meant if I scooted in the back today, I would have to do the same for the next six weeks. Ugh!

I didn't like that idea. Montu is younger than me. It didn't seem right that I should give him my seat. Maybe I could suggest that we take turns sitting in the middle. That was only fair.

Kavita leaned forward. "I think you should talk to Mom and Dad about it."

"Maybe," I said, but I wasn't going to.

She was busy chewing her food. It gave me an opportunity to think.

---

**Op-por-tu-ni-ty** means a special chance to do something you wish or like to do.

---

I made a list, of course!

In-my-head list of why I didn't want

to ask Mom and Dad about the seating

arrangements

33

* They are always telling us that we have to treat our guests nicely.

* That means they would probably say that I should give up my seat for Montu.

* Once they say that, I have to do it.

* If I don't ask, I might have a chance to keep my seat.

* If I keep my seat, I will get to sit next to Mom or Dadi for their whole visit.

* If Mom and Dad asks us to take turns it would still be better than having to ride in the back for the next six weeks.

"I won't ask Mom and Dad where I should sit in the van right now," I told Kavita. "I don't want to burden them."

"What does 'burden' mean?"

"'Burden' means you give someone too much to take care of. They already have a lot to worry about."

The look on her face was clear. She didn't believe me. But Kavita didn't have time to ask more questions, because Mom came into the kitchen, showered and dressed. "If you're done with breakfast, put your dishes up, change your clothes, and comb your hair, please."

Kavita and I did what Mom asked us to do. When we returned, Dad was at the kitchen sink, washing his hands.

"Are you ready to leave?" he asked. "I want to be on the road by ten."

Dadi and Montu were arriving at four o'clock. The drive to the airport would take about three hours. If we left at ten, we would get to the airport around one. Then we would have to wait for three more hours!

"Dad, why're we going so early?" I asked.

"Okay, let me explain," he said. "Yes, it takes three hours to get to O'Hare. But then we have to allow an hour for a flat tire or maybe some other problems that might occur. We also need to add an hour in case there are traffic delays due to accidents or construction. And then we should also plan an hour for lunch, bathroom breaks, and getting gas. So, three hours extra is what we need."

I made a quick calculation in my head: 3 hours for driving + 1 hour for car trouble + 1 hour for traffic + 1 hour for lunch, bathroom, and gas.

All of that meant we needed

$3 + 1 + 1 + 1 = 6$ hours

10:00 a.m. + 6 hours = 4:00 p.m.

I handed Dad a towel. "But we might not have any problems. We could eat lunch at home, leave at noon, and still get there in time."

"If Dadi and Montu get there before us they might panic," Dad said. "They've never been here, and we want to make sure we're there to welcome them as soon as they come out of the gate."

Mom grabbed two extra jackets from the closet.

"Why are you taking those?" I asked her.

"These are for Dadi and Montu. They come from a

warm place, and the weather here might feel quite chilly to them. I doubt they have the right clothing."

I nodded.

When we got into the van, Kavita didn't say anything about our seating arrangements.

> Ar-range-ments means how we put things or people in their proper place.

Phew!

***

"Nina, Nina, let's go," Kavita nudged me. I had fallen asleep.

"Are we there?"

"No," Mom replied. "An hour more to go."

"Then I want to stay in the van." I closed my eyes again.

"Nina, we're stopping to get doughnuts."

I certainly wanted a doughnut.

Mom glanced at her watch. "You know, we have a lot of time. We should eat inside, not in the van while we drive."

"But we don't want to be late," Dad said.

"It is only noon," Mom said. "Besides, I don't want powdered sugar all over the seats. If ants get in, it will be a problem."

"Okay," Dad agreed.

I was still groggy, but my blueberry doughnut and milk woke me up. It is the best snack ever.

Even with our doughnut break, we reached the airport before 1:30—more than two hours early. There were many people like us who were waiting for their visitors. Luckily, after we parked the van and went into the airport, we found empty seats near the gates where Dadi and Montu would come out.

Each time a flight arrived people rushed forward to greet their friends or family. I watched all the hugging, crying, laughing, and talking. Finally, I grew bored.

"Dad, we came way too early," I said.

"Yes, but if our van had broken down or if we had a flat tire, we would have made it right on time." Dad snapped his fingers like he'd just thought of something. "Anyway, their flight might get here early."

"Not a chance." I pointed at the monitor. "Look at the arrival time. It's twenty minutes late."

"What?" He rushed over to the monitor.

When he returned, he paced back and forth around our seats, rubbing his palms together. I made an in-my-head list of why Dad might be so jumpy. I mean, he was almost bouncing like a little kid.

* This is the first time Dad's mom and nephew have come from India.

* He thought of so many things that might go wrong, but none of them did.

* He had not thought of one thing: that the flight might be late.

* Now he realized that we really had come too early.

✱ Maybe he was tired and hungry. (He hadn't

even finished his doughnut earlier.)

"Dad, would you like a piece of gum?" I asked.

"Sure."

I passed it to him.

"Thanks," he said.

Dad unwrapped the gum and put it in his mouth. Maybe chewing used up some of his energy, because his pacing slowed down.

✱✱✱

As soon as Dadi and Montu's flight was announced, I shook Kavita. "Wake up. They've landed."

"Yay!" She looked around. "Where are they?"

"They still have to go through customs," Mom said.

"What's customs?" Kavita asked.

"When you travel to another country, you have to show your passport and explain why you're visiting," Mom replied.

"What's a passport?" Kavita asked.

"It is an official notebook that shows where you're from and which other countries you've visited," I explained. I know all about it because we made passports in second grade when we pretend-traveled to other countries. "We also have them because we traveled to India."

"You're right, Nina," Dad said.

"You also have to tell them if you've brought anything with you that might be a problem, like plants or fruits," I said.

"Why?"

"So they don't bring any plant disease from another country."

"What if you bring stuff and don't tell them?"

"You get in trouble if you get caught," Mom said.

Kavita shook her head. "That's too many things to do before we see them."

"Let's just get ready, Kavita."

Kavita and I unrolled the welcome sign and stood behind the barricade, Dad and Mom behind us.

Dadi and Montu came through the glass doors with their luggage!

Kavita began jumping.

That made it hard to hold on to the sign and it ripped.

I took a deep breath. It was almost time to be Nina Soni, Perfect Hostess.

But did I want to give up my seat in the van to Montu? Did I want to give up my room to Dadi and Montu?

Then they were with us, and all my doubts were gone.

Dadi hugged me. "It's been such a long time, Nina!" Her eyes were moist.

Montu looked around. "I can't believe I am here! It's like a dream."

Kavita pinched him.

"Why did you do that?" he asked.

"So you know you're not dreaming."

He laughed.

We stepped outside and Dadi shivered. Dad handed her and Montu the extra jackets and they put them on. Then we went out to the parking deck. Dad and Mom loaded the luggage into the van.

"Montu, do you want to get in the back with me?" Kavita asked.

"If you promise not to pinch me again."

"I won't." She climbed into the van. He followed.

Phew! I didn't have to give up my seat.

Mom opened the front door for Dadi. "Please get in."

"You sit up in front, Lalita. I would like to ride with Nina," she replied.

I was the hostess and supposed to be kind, but I realized a guest (Dadi) could be kind too.

## CHAPTER FOUR

Kavita and Montu whispered to each other on the drive back home. Dad and Mom asked Dadi about everyone they knew in India. There are more than a billion people in India, so it was a long list. On top of that, they spoke in Hindi, so fast that I couldn't catch a word. A few times Montu chimed in. I thought I knew Hindi well, but I was wrong. I couldn't follow several people speaking at once.

I stared out the window for a while, but there wasn't much to see. Everyone was entertaining our guests except for me. I hadn't even had a chance to be a hostess yet.

From the corner of my eye, I saw Dadi glance at me. She put her hand up. "We will talk later," she said to Mom and Dad. "Now I want to talk to my eldest grandchild."

How did she know that I was feeling lonely?

"Nina," Dadi said, "I wanted to see this country even before your parents came here. And after they did, I was sure I would visit someday."

I couldn't believe Dadi had been waiting so long to visit the United States. "But they moved here fifteen years ago!"

"Yes." She took my hand and kissed it. "And today more than my dream has come true."

I looked at her. "What do you mean?"

"At that time," Dadi said, "I had not thought about having three precious grandchildren. Now I get to see this country with Montu, be with my son and daughter-in-law, and spend time with you and Kavita."

"Now that you're finally here"—I laced my fingers in hers—"what would you like to do the most?"

"Let's see." She tapped her chin with her finger. "I want

to see and enjoy your house and garden. We can go on walks in the neighborhood and meet your friends. I would like to spend time with Jay. I have heard so much about him that I feel like I already know him."

I nodded. "You'll certainly see Jay and his parents, Meera Masi and Uncle Ryan. Would you like to go to some of our favorite restaurants?"

"Yes. I also look forward to grocery shopping and visiting a garden center." Dadi beamed. "I would like to do all the things that you do. Is that silly?"

"No, but you may not want to do *everything* we have to do. Like go to the dentist or the doctor."

She laughed. "That's right. Unless I have a toothache or I am sick, I will skip the dentist and the doctor."

"We will do some special, super-fun things. Like visit the lakes and go to the Olbrich Gardens."

"That would be wonderful."

I pointed out the window and read the sign out loud. "Welcome to Wisconsin."

"Weren't we already in Wisconsin?" Montu asked.

"No, no, Montu. O'Hare is in Illinois," Kavita said. "You have already been in two states."

"That means I only have forty-eight more to go!"

I was impressed that Montu knew there are fifty states. He must have prepared before they left.

"Am I right?" he asked loudly.

"Yes," Kavita said, and added, "Please use your inside voice."

"But we're outside," he said.

"We are not *outside* outside. We are inside the van, so we have to use our inside voices."

Montu covered his face. "Everybody is always telling me that!"

Dadi turned to look at him. "You know the reason why."

"Montu, when I was your age, everyone used to tell me that too," Dad said.

"I'm just like you!" Montu smiled like that was the best thing ever. "How much longer?"

"Not long," Dad said. "There hasn't been much traffic, so we made pretty good time."

"Just think, Montu," Kavita said, "we had to drive and drive this morning to come to the airport to get you."

"And I had to fly and fly to visit you."

"But flying is amazing." Kavita flapped her arms. "You feel like a bird."

"A bird in a cage."

They both giggled. I didn't know what was so funny.

I pointed at a sign. "Forty miles to Madison."

"That is how many kilometers?" Montu asked.

"I don't know," I replied.

"One mile is approximately 1.6 kilometers," Dadi said.

I calculated.

First, I took 1.6 and made it 1 and .6.

Then I did some multiplication.

40 miles x 1 = 40 kilometers

40 miles x .6 = 24 kilometers

40 + 24 = 64 kilometers

At the same time, Montu and I each said "64!" How had he come up with the right answer so quickly?

When we pulled into our driveway, Dadi's eyes grew moist. Again. She stepped out of the van and looked around. She sniffed. "Is there jasmine blooming?"

"No." But I thought I knew what she was talking about, so I took her hand and led her to the end of our driveway. I pointed to the shrubs with purple flowers.

Dadi leaned forward, closed her eyes, and breathed deeply. Then she opened them and examined the flowers.

"Aren't those four petals perfectly symmetrical?" I asked.

"They are, and so delicate! Ever wonder where the flowers hide their sweet perfume?"

"I never thought about it."

"I didn't either until today," she said. "What is this plant called?"

"Lilac. It comes in four colors: dark purple, light purple, magenta pink, and white."

"You certainly know your flowers," Dadi said. "Thank you for introducing me to lilacs."

I felt good about doing my hostess duty and showing her new things.

While Dad and Mom took the luggage inside, Montu and Kavita chased each other around the yard. Dadi pointed at a yellow flower. "Did you plant that in the middle of the lawn?"

"That's a dandelion," I answered. "It's a weed. They pop up in spring without planting. And they can spread very fast."

"You mean you give them a finger and they bite off your entire hand?"

It took me a minute to understand what she was saying. "Yes. You give it a little and it takes a lot."

"All the luggage is unloaded," Mom said. "Are you two coming in?"

I guessed everyone else had gone inside already, so we did too.

I looked around the kitchen. "Where are Kavita and Montu?"

"Kavita has taken him for the grand tour of the house," Mom said.

The basement door was open, and the light was on. I should have guessed that Kavita would want to show off the basement, because she always wants to talk about the haunted tunnel we once built.

Just because Montu and Kavita rode in the back seat together, she didn't have to claim him. Then I realized I had claimed Dadi in the same way.

> **Claim** means to say that a person or a thing is yours. All yours.

I wanted to be a perfect hostess, but I also needed to be a fair older sister.

"Would you like to shower first?" Mom asked Dadi.

"Yes. It will melt away half of my tiredness."

"Mom, can I take her upstairs please?" I asked.

"Certainly. Make sure you show her how the shower works."

"OK," I replied, but I was confused. I haven't had to show Priya and her family how to operate the shower.

---

**Op-er-ate** means to make something work, like a car or a vacuum cleaner or even a shower.

---

I led Dadi upstairs to my room.

"This used to be mine, but now you and Montu are going to sleep here," I said. I felt like a proper hostess.

"Thank you for giving us your room. Where will you sleep?"

"Kavita will share her room with me while you're here."

"That is nice of you both." Dadi looked around. "Your room is large, but it will be hard to share that small bed with Montu."

I thought she was joking, but she looked serious.

"That's a trundle bed," I said.

Now she looked confused. "What's that?"

I pulled the bottom bed out. She clapped her hands. "That's perfect. This way Montu and I won't be fighting for space or blankets."

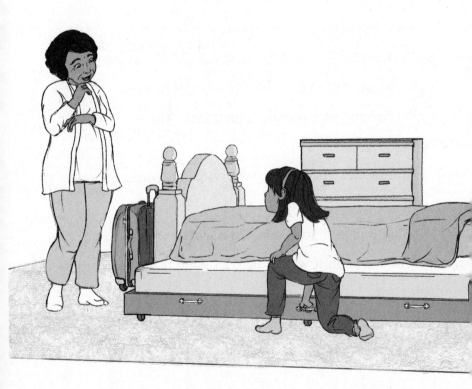

I took her to the bathroom and turned the faucet in the shower. "If you want hot water, you turn it left, or if you want colder, you turn it right."

"That's simple. How long before the water heats up?"

Now I was confused. I put my hand in the water. "See, it's already warm."

"Oh," Dadi said. "I heard that hot water comes out instantly here, but I forgot about it. It takes longer in India."

Mom poked her head in. "How is it going?"

"Nina is doing a perfect job," Dadi said.

"One more thing." I handed her the set of towels Kavita had picked for her.

"While Dadi takes her shower, will you help me?" Mom asked me.

"Sure." I went downstairs with Mom. Kavita and Montu were sitting at the dining table.

"I love your basement," Montu said. "This is the first time I've seen one."

Kavita eyes filled with surprise. "You had never ever seen a basement before?"

"Nobody I know in India has a basement," he said. "Can we play down there sometimes?"

Montu was our guest. If I wanted to be a perfect hostess, shouldn't I do what he wanted to do? But we also had to follow our family rule. "When it's nice weather, my parents want us to play outside," I said. "We can spend time in the basement when it rains or when it is dark."

Montu moved his head in a tiny circle. "Sure!" he said.

"Why are you moving your head like an Indian puppet?" Kavita asked.

Montu looked puzzled. "You mean like a kathputli?"

"Yes. If you agree with Nina, you should move your head up and down like this." Kavita nodded. "Not in a circle." She tried to copy him, but it looked really funny.

Mom said, "Kavita, what Montu did may not look like nodding to you, but it sure is. That's the way people nod in India."

"I want to learn Montu-nodding," Kavita said.

He couldn't stop giggling. I joined him even though I didn't want to laugh at Kavita. I thought she might get mad, but she kept practicing.

Dadi called from the top of the stairs, "Montu, time for you to take a shower."

"You have been traveling for many hours, Montu. Soap and scrub yourself well." Mom put a dish in the microwave. "As soon as you're done with the shower, we'll eat."

"Are we having pizza for dinner?" he asked.

"Not tonight. But we can have it tomorrow."

"Thank you."

"You have never had pizza before?" I asked him.

"I have. But only in India. I always wanted to try American pizza." He ran upstairs.

Kavita sat at the table. "I like Montu. I think we will keep him as long as he wants to stay."

*He's going to spend his entire vacation here even if you don't like him,* I thought, but all I said was, "He is nice."

"And a little giggly, right?" she whispered.

"Giggles are better than tears," I said. I laid down six place mats. Then I took out six glasses and six plates. "Can you get the napkins?"

Kavita brought four of them to the table.

"We need more than that. There are four of us plus Dadi and Montu."

"Four plus one is five and five plus one is six." Kavita counted on her fingers.

"Great addition," I said. "We should set up everything before our guests come down."

Kavita got two more napkins. "I wonder if they are our guests or family," she said as she folded them in half.

"I'm not sure," I said. "But they have just arrived, so they still very much feel like guests to me."

I made an in-my-head list.

* Montu had asked for pizza just like Kavita or I would.

* Usually, guests don't ask for what they want to eat. Only close friends and family do.

* Mom also told Montu to soap and scrub well. Usually, she doesn't do that to kids who are guests.

* Maybe that's why Montu wasn't shy about asking for pizza. He knows he is with family.

* But he doesn't live here all the time. He is going back to his home in a few weeks. Doesn't that make him a guest?

* Also, he has traveled all the way from India. Even if he is family, everything is different for him here, like it would be for a guest.

All this thinking made my brain tangle up. "Let's not worry about it now."

Kavita moved her head as if she were a puppet. "Okay." Then she asked, "Am I Montu-nodding?"

Maybe in six weeks Kavita would be able to nod just like Montu, but she hadn't mastered it yet. "You're getting better."

## CHAPTER FIVE

"Today, we're going to visit the Olbrich Gardens," Mom announced at breakfast the next morning.

"May I invite Jay?" I asked.

"That's a great idea." Mom passed me a platter of khakhra Dadi had brought from India. "Let me call Meera Masi."

"Nina, he's your friend, right?" Montu asked.

"He certainly is."

"Don't forget he's my friend too," Kavita added.

I wondered if Jay had ever tried khakhra. It is basically a toasted roti. It is crisp like a cracker or a potato chip. I had eaten khakhra before, but not homemade ones. They were delicious.

We had just finished breakfast when Jay came over. I introduced him to Montu and Dadi. Dadi gave Jay a hug and he looked kind of surprised. I was too.

"Your dadi is just like my patti," Jay whispered when we were alone. "Always giving hugs."

Jay calls his grandmother Patti. It means "grandma" in Tamil. Tamil is an Indian language that Jay's mom speaks the way Mom and Dad speak Hindi. India is a big country and there are many different languages spoken there.

"Then why did you look shocked when she hugged you?" I opened the khakhra container and offered him some. "You should have expected it."

He took two and put them on a plate. "I should have." He sat down and started eating. "At least she didn't ruffle my hair."

"Is that what your patti does?" I asked.

He nodded.

Montu and Kavita rushed in. "Time to go."

Jay finished the last bite and took his dish to the sink. "That was wonderful. Thanks," he said.

We all got in the van. Jay sat in the back with Kavita and Montu. I wondered why he did that. Was he afraid of Dadi's hugs? Did he want to be with Kavita and Montu? Was he sitting in the back so I didn't have to? I didn't ask him, though.

During the ride Dad gave a running commentary.

Com-men-tar-y means an explanation or a description of something that you're seeing.

Dad said, "That's a mall. On the left is the middle school and the high school. The street we're on is Mineral Point Road. Now we just crossed Whitney Way. We're heading east, getting closer to the University of Wisconsin."

That's when I realized Dad was not taking the beltline, which is the faster way to get to the Olbrich Gardens. Instead, he was going right through the city so he could point out every little thing. That meant his commentary would last the whole ride. I settled back in my seat and let Dad take over the hosting.

Finally, we reached the gardens and Dad parked the van. It was a perfect day to be outdoors. As we entered the garden, I glanced around. I made an in-my-head list of all the things I could see.

* There were flower beds filled with tulips in shades of yellow, red, and white. Some were deep purple, the color of the night sky. Those flowers were regal.

* Daffodils nodded in the breeze, looking as happy as I felt.

* The hyacinths smelled like a lady with too much perfume on.

* And of course, as soon as you walked by the lilac shrubs you were surrounded by a sweet scent—milder than the hyacinths.

* The crab apple trees were covered with flowers—some white, others light pink, and still others with dark pink blossoms.

We could see all these plants and flowers, and we hadn't even explored the entire garden!

**Ex-plore** means to study, travel, or go over something.

"I have only seen gardens like this in pictures," Dadi said dreamily. "I don't know what any of the plants are."

"I'll tell you what they are," I said. "And we can ask Mom about the ones I don't know."

"Wonderful," she said.

Mom was by a large pot filled with blue flowers. She gestured for Dadi to come over.

"I'll be right back, partner," Dadi said and walked away.

Montu reached out for my hand. "Can I go with you two?" he asked Jay and me.

Jay glanced at me. Kavita's face fell. I guessed that she didn't want to be left out. But the path was too narrow for all four of us to walk together.

What should I do? I looked for help. Dadi and Mom were still studying the potted plant and Dad was nowhere in sight. He was probably picking up a map of the gardens at the front desk. Dad likes to study all the handouts. He is a software engineer and always wants to have a plan before he does anything.

I had invited Jay to come with us, so I felt like I needed to stay with him. But Montu was also a guest. How could I be a perfect hostess to both of them? I thought about how Kavita and Montu had enjoyed being together so far. That meant Kavita was also a good hostess.

"Maybe you and Kavita can walk with my mom and dad," I said to Montu. "I can stay with Jay and Dadi. That way Kavita and I will each be with at least one of our guests."

"Guests?" Montu asked. "Who are your guests?"

"You are one of them, silly," Kavita said.

Montu folded his arms. "No, I am not."

"You're visiting, so you're a guest. Right?" I said.

"Nope. I am just family," Montu insisted.

---

**In-sist** means to think what you believe is right and to want everyone else to believe it too.

---

"I'm a guest," Jay said, and looked Montu in the eyes. "It's better to be a guest than a host or a family member. Everyone has to treat a guest nicely."

After a few seconds Montu said, "Accha, I want to be a guest like Jay."

"Accha" means "okay" or "good," so Montu was agreeing with Jay.

Dad came out of the building with the map. Just as I had guessed. "Dad!" I waved my hand. "Over here."

"Got it." He waved the map. "Now we're ready."

"We've been here a hundred times, Dad. We don't need a map."

"I do," he said. "Now, group one is you, Jay, and Dadi, and group two is Kavita, Montu, Mom, and me."

I couldn't have been happier.

Our group walked ahead and group two followed. But that only lasted for a while. Montu and Kavita ran ahead to sit on every bench and then chased each other. Before I knew it Dadi was back with Mom and Dad, and Jay and I were alone. I wanted to be with Dadi, but she moved slowly, stopping and reading the name of each plant. *She is going to be with us for six weeks*, I thought. *I'll have plenty of time to spend with her.*

"So much for two groups. Now we're three groups," I said to Jay. "Two pairs and one group of three."

"And when we all stop to look at something at the same time, there are seven of us," he said.

"This is a rose garden," I heard Mom say to Dadi as she pointed to a large area with many shrubs.

"Where are the flowers?" Dadi asked. "Without blossoms they're just thorny shrubs. Not a pretty sight."

"It's too early," I said. "Roses bloom in June here."

"Did you know that when I was little it was my job to pluck flowers for my grandmother's puja?" Dadi asked.

Puja is a special prayer. "Did she do puja every day?"

"Yes. Every morning, right after my bath, I went out with a basket and plucked flowers."

"Like tulips, and daffodils, and roses?" Jay asked.

"Not daffodils and tulips. They don't grow in India except maybe in the north. I grew up in a town near Mumbai, in the southwestern part of the country."

He smiled. "Then what other flowers did you pick?"

"Oh, plumeria, hibiscus, jasmine."

"Do you still pick flowers for puja, Dadi?" I asked.

She shook her head. "In Mumbai I don't have a garden. I do my puja without flowers."

"Is that even a puja?" I asked.

"Puja can be done however you want it," Dadi

explained. "The important part is to have faith and devotion."

"My mom lights a lamp after her shower and recites shlokas," Jay said. "She even sings a couple of them when she says good night to me."

Shlokas are Sanskrit prayers. I thought I knew everything about Jay, since he's my best friend, but I was wrong. I didn't know Meera Masi sang shlokas to him every night.

"What is your favorite thing in these gardens?" Montu asked me.

"The lilac and hyacinth flowers, because they smell so good," I said.

"What about you, Kavita?"

Kavita pointed at the red-and-gold structure ahead of us. "The Thai Pavilion is my favorite because I think it looks like a palace."

Montu turned to Jay. "What is your favorite part?"

"I don't know," Jay said. "The entire garden."

"You have to pick one thing."

"No, I don't." Jay sounded irritated.

"Yes, you do." Montu's voice was shrill.

What could I do? They were both my guests. Should I tell Jay to pick one thing or ask Montu to back off? Or we could stop talking and avoid an argument. As a hostess I had to try to keep everyone calm.

I said, "Montu, Jay likes everything. Isn't that great?"

"No. He has to choose one thing."

"Well," Kavita said. "You can't make him do that if he doesn't want to. You're not the boss of him."

"But. . . but. . . I'm a guest," Montu said. "Jay has to do what I say."

"Nope. You're our guest, not Jay's." Kavita folded her arms.

"And don't forget, he's our guest too," I said.

Dad told us to hurry up, which was good. It distracted Montu, at least for the moment.

"What is *your* favorite thing in the whole garden?" Montu asked Mom.

She pointed at a woody vine climbing up the brick wall. "I like that hydrangea."

Montu squinted at the tiny leaves. "You like that twisty thing?"

"Right now, it doesn't look like much," Mom said, "but when it blooms it's covered with white flowers. It's beautiful."

"Oh!" Montu turned to Dad. "What about you?"

"The ice-cream bars." He pointed at the door. "They sell them inside."

"Ice cream!" Montu covered his mouth as if to muffle his voice.

"Isn't it too early and too cold for ice cream?" Dadi asked.

"It's past noon," Dad said. "We'll visit the conservatory first. It's warm in there."

Bolz Conservatory is a huge greenhouse filled with tropical plants and trees. At the front desk I picked up a list of plants and a pencil. The trees and plants were labeled so we could make sure we'd seen them all.

"Can I hold the list?" Montu asked.

I gave it to him.

"This place feels as warm as India," Dadi said.

"Do you like it?" I asked.

She took off her shawl. "I do."

We found acacia, papaya, coffee, plumeria, and many others. None of these plants can survive outside in the Wisconsin winter, which is why they are kept under a huge glass dome.

**Sur-vive** means to stay alive.

We left the conservatory and entered the main building. I said, "Here is where we get ice cream, Dadi."

"I'm warmer now, so I'm ready for it."

Jay and I took our ice cream outside and sat on a garden bench. "Kavita stood up for you, Jay," I said.

"You both did," he said. "When Kavita said, 'you're not the boss of him,' Montu was speechless."

"Well, he deserved that." I took another bite of ice

cream and was quiet for a moment. "I've been trying to decide if Dadi and Montu are family or guests. What do you think?"

"Nina, what difference does it make?"

"I guess it doesn't matter."

"Just don't . . ." Jay seemed to be searching for a word.

"Overthink?"

He grinned. "You nailed it."

"Thanks, Jay," I said sarcastically. "I was just trying to figure things out."

He took a last bite of his ice cream and crumpled the wrapper. He extended his hand and I gave him mine too. He walked over to the garbage can and threw them away.

Sometimes, Jay and I understand each other without even talking. Like right now. When he put his hand out, I knew what he was asking for.

It was easy to be with Mom, Dad, Kavita, and Jay. Dadi was a guest, but I was comfortable with her. Would Montu always be a bit challenging?

On the drive home Montu asked, "Dadi, what did you like the best?"

"I'm happy that I was able to visit such a beautiful garden with my grandchildren, Jay, and my son and daughter-in-law," Dadi said.

"That's not just one thing."

"Sometimes," Dadi said, "we like more than one thing."

"I guess," Montu replied.

I wondered why Montu had to ask everyone what we liked best. Was it that he wanted to have the chance to tell us what he enjoyed the most? Maybe that was it. A good hostess figures out the needs of their guests without them asking for it. I hoped I was doing that.

"What did you like the best?" I asked Montu.

"Ice cream!"

## CHAPTER SIX

That night we made pizza, just like Montu had requested. He watched us roll out the dough for a bit and then borrowed Dadi's phone to take a video. He filmed Kavita spreading the sauce on the crust and me shredding the cheese.

"If you want to eat pizza, you must help make it, Montu," Kavita said. "You can't just make videos."

"But I have never done it before."

"There's always a first time." I handed him a bowl of olives. "You can put these on our pizza."

"Can I taste one first to see if I like it?"

"Sure," I said.

Kavita sang, *"Olives, olives, plump and pretty, you are delicious green or black."*

"I love them," Montu said. "The black one is salty and the green one is salty and sour." Montu scattered the olives on top of the sauce. Then the three of us sprinkled cheese on the pizzas.

Our pizza came out of the oven first, so we ate before the grown-ups. Kavita and I watched Montu take his first bite. He chewed and chewed as if he was trying to figure out the taste.

"Don't you like it?" Kavita asked.

He chewed some more and then swallowed. "I do," he said, but I wasn't sure if he meant it. His "yes" was mushy like Jell-O, not crisp like a khakhra. I think he was just trying to be polite.

---

**Po-lite** means to try to be nice or careful about not hurting someone's feelings.

---

"Does American pizza taste different from Indian pizza?" I asked.

"Yes," Montu said. "American pizza is too sour."

"Maybe you put too many green olives on it," I said.

He shook his head. "In India I even put raw mango pieces on mine. They're very sour. I think it's the sauce. Indian pizza sauce is sweeter than American."

I tried to be polite and not show what I thought about sweet tomato sauce. Instead, I tried to be helpful. I opened the sugar bowl. "Want to sprinkle a little sugar on it?"

"Thanks." He took a spoonful of sugar and sprinkled it over his pizza, then took a bite. "Yum," he said. "That's perfect!"

Kavita sang, *"Let's turn American pizza into an Indian pizza. Just add sugar and make it sweet."*

"Try it, Nina. You'll love it," Montu said. "Guaranteed."

The thought of sugar on my pizza didn't sound good at all. "No, thanks."

"Kavita?" Montu asked.

"Not me." She shook her head. "I like American pizza."

"But you're Indian," he said. "You'll like Indian pizza."

"But I'm also American and I love this pizza."

Montu slid the sugar bowl toward Kavita. "You were born in America but you're still Indian."

"No, we're Indian American," she announced.

"You eat dal and roti and other stuff we eat in India. You know Hindi. We have the same grandparents and you look like me," Montu said. "That means you are Indian."

"It doesn't matter what we eat or speak or who we look like," I said. "Americans come from all over the world."

"The United States is a melding pot. Right, Nina?" Kavita said.

She had said "a melding pot" instead of "a melting pot," but I thought that worked too. Melding and melting are similar—individual things combined into a whole.

Why were we even talking about this? I made a quick in-my-head list to try to sort out my thoughts.

* Kavita and I are American because we were born here. We have always lived in this country. The United States is our home.
* We eat a lot of Indian food, like Montu does.
* We speak Hindi (not as well as he does, though).
* We play Indian music and sometimes we wear Indian clothes the same way he does.
* We celebrate Indian festivals and holidays.
* Montu is from India. We are his cousins, and we look and act like him. To him, this means that we are Indian.
* But we are Indian American.

"You're right, Kavita," I said. "We have Indian heritage but we're American. Lots of Americans have their roots in other countries, but they're still Americans."

Kavita nodded, not like Montu but in her up-and-down American way.

"What does 'heritage' mean?" Montu asked.

"'Heritage' means 'background,'" I said. "Kavita and I have Indian heritage because our family is from India. Someone like Jay has two different backgrounds because his mother's family is from India and his father's family is from Norway and Britain."

"Accha, I get it," Montu said.

I wasn't sure if he really did.

Kavita sang, *"Indian Americans are Indian and American, two for the price of one. Sorry, but we are not for sale!"*

Montu laughed. Kavita had such a way of making him feel good. I wished I could be like that.

"Now let's just eat," I said.

Montu picked up his sweet Indian pizza and we ate our sour American pizza.

Yummy!

## CHAPTER SEVEN

Montu was waiting for us in the front yard when we got home from school on Monday. "You're here!" he shouted.

"Yup! We're ready to hang out with you," Kavita said.

Montu looked confused. "What does 'hang out' mean?"

"To spend time with you," I said.

"I like that."

"What did you do all day, Montu?" I asked.

"Not much." He shrugged. "I read, played, and took a nap. Oh, and I met Mr. and Mrs. Crump. They're nice."

"They're the best. They always call us by our names," Kavita said.

He looked puzzled so I explained, "Some people have a hard time saying our Indian names, but not the Crumps."

"Accha."

While I did my homework, Montu and Kavita played outside. I watched them through the window bouncing a ball. Then they took out hula-hoops. Montu tried to keep his spinning and burst out laughing.

Someone put a hand on my shoulder. It was Dadi.

"Doesn't he look silly?" I asked.

"They both look equally silly." She glanced at my books. "Do you have a lot of schoolwork?"

I sighed. "I do."

By the time I finished, Montu and Kavita had come inside. I thought about asking if they wanted to go outside with me now that I was done, but Montu looked so tired that I didn't say anything.

He yawned. "Are we eating soon, Dadi?"

"Not for a while. Are you hungry?"

"I'm sleepy."

"Try to stay awake for a while," Dadi said. "Maybe you can play a board game."

Kavita ran upstairs and got Chutes and Ladders.

While we played, Montu could barely keep his eyes open. We ate as soon as Dad came home.

Montu went to bed right after dinner. It wasn't even six o'clock! It was two more hours until my bedtime.

Dadi stayed up a little bit longer and tried to teach me Hindi numbers. I already knew how to count to ten out loud, so now I was learning to write the numbers.

1, 2, 3, 4, 5, 6, 7, 8, 9, 10

ek, do, teen, chaar, paanch, chay, saath, aanth, nou, dus

१ २ ३ ४ ५ ६ ७ ८ ९ १०

But she kept dozing off. I guessed they were both still kind of jet-lagged.

> **Jet-lagged** means after you travel through different time zones and feel very tired.

India is on the other side of the globe, so Dadi's and Montu's nights and days were turned around. Mom said it would take them a few days to get accustomed to the time in Madison.

> **Ac-cus-tom** means get used to a new custom.

**✳✳✳**

On Friday, Montu was not waiting for us when we got home. Kavita sang, *"Montu, Montu, where are you? Say it loud so I can join you! No more school for the next two days. So we can play, play, play."*

"I'm in my room!" he hollered. "I'm working on a puzzle."

She raced upstairs.

"I'm going to finish a little bit of work," Mom said. "Dadi is waiting for you in the kitchen."

"She is?" One part of me wanted to go upstairs with

Kavita and Montu, but I also wondered what Dadi had planned for us. I went into the kitchen.

"What are you making?" I asked. "Can I help?"

"Do you want your snack?"

"Is it okay if I cook first? I'm not that hungry. Kavita went upstairs, so she must not be either."

"Wash your hands and I'll show you how to make gajar halwa."

"Gajar" means "carrots" in Hindi and halwa is a sweet; gajar halwa is a dessert made with carrots. I have had it at an Indian restaurant but never a homemade version.

"Is it difficult to make?" I asked.

"The only big chore is grating."

"I can do that. I grate cheese all the time."

"I saw that when we had pizza. You're good at it." Dadi gave me a grater. "Be careful."

I began shredding carrots and she chopped dates.

"How much grated carrot do we need?" I asked.

"Two cups."

I piled everything I'd shredded in a measuring cup. There was a little leftover, so I ate it.

Dadi heated ghee, which is clarified butter, in a glass dish in the microwave. When it melted, she added the dates and then I dumped in the carrots.

"Will you stir it?" she asked.

"Sure."

The orange carrots and the dark brown dates looked delicious all swirled together.

Dadi added cardamom, milk, and homemade cheese. Then she placed it back in the microwave for a few minutes.

When she took it out, steam rose from the half-cooked halwa. I breathed it in. "It smells good."

"Wait until you taste it."

"When do you think I'll be able to make this on my own?" I asked.

"Soon, I suppose. But it's up to your parents. They know when you're ready to handle cooking by yourself."

"Do you think we can have it for snack?"

"Why not?" Dadi said. "Tell me all about your day."

She washed strawberries while I took out small bowls.

Dadi put a berry in her mouth. "Delicious!"

I sat at the table. "My friend Megan is coming over on Sunday to work on our book reports. We're in different classes and are doing our own projects, but we thought it would be fun to work together *and* talk."

"Accha." Dadi's eyes crinkled. I wondered if it was because the strawberries were so tasty or if she knew Megan and I were going work a little, talk a lot.

"It's not due for two weeks so I think we have time," I said. "Anyway, it's nice to do something together."

"You mean to have an excuse to do something together." She laughed. "What about Jay?"

"Jay is busy this weekend," I said. I didn't tell Dadi that he had invited me to join him. She might feel bad that I didn't go because she and Montu were visiting. I think a perfect hostess wouldn't mention that. I added, "But we will see him at a dance class next week."

"I see." Dadi stirred the gajar halwa mixture.

The smell of cardamom was making me hungry. "In the spring Jay goes fishing with his Grandpa Joe and his cousin Jeff a lot."

"I'm sure you miss him. Do you think you would like to go fishing with him?"

"No." I wrinkled my nose. "I don't want to sit around waiting for a fish to bite."

"Have you even done it?"

"No. It sounds boring, and it might be smelly."

"I'm sure you don't say that to Jay."

"I never do."

She put the bowl back in the microwave and turned it on again. "It is almost ready." She looked thoughtful. "I suppose it is not just fishing but being with his grandpa and cousin that makes this activity enjoyable for Jay."

I didn't tell Dadi that sometimes I was jealous that Jay could see his grandpa and cousins anytime he wanted. "I guess so."

"It is difficult to have our family so far away, isn't it?"

How did Dadi know what I was feeling? I could not stop the tears that were prickling my eyes.

She pressed my hand. Her eyes were wet too.

She missed us as much as we missed her. And that's why she understood my feelings.

The microwave beeped again.

"Time to eat." Dadi took out the dish. "Could you please call everyone?"

The five of us shared the gajar halwa that Dadi and I had made. We saved some for Dad too.

But Dadi and I didn't share our talks. They were just for us.

*❋❋❋*

On Saturday Dadi got out some Hindi books. "Now that you can count to ten, let's do some writing."

Writing Hindi is almost like doing artwork. The letters in the alphabet are curvy, and I struggled to get the shapes right. Also, in English there are only 26 letters in the alphabet but in Hindi there are many more. That meant it would take longer to learn them all.

I tried to pay attention, but my mind wandered off. Mom had taken Kavita and Montu to the grocery. Would she let him buy all the treats he wanted like he was a guest? Or would she tell him to pick one thing, the way she does with us? What would Montu pick? I hoped he got ice cream or maybe some chocolates. I kept looking out the window to see if they were back.

"You seem distracted. Take a couple of deep breaths and tame your thoughts. That's the only way to learn something new," Dadi said.

I tried to do what she had said. I felt calmer.

The only problem was that my calmness didn't last too long. When I first learned the English alphabet, I had a difficult time with the lowercase letters *b* and *d*. In Hindi, there were many more letters that I kept messing up or combining into something new.

I wrote the letter that I thought made the sound of *T*.

Dadi pointed out, "You did *T* but I see you have added part of *K* to it just for fun."

"This is difficult," I sighed.

"Nina, drop by drop a lake gets filled," she said.

"What do you mean?"

"It may seem like you are only adding a drop to your Hindi, that you are only learning a tiny bit, but each lesson will make you better and better. Until you have mastered it," she explained.

"There is so much to learn. I still haven't even started on lowercase letters."

"There is no upper or lower in Hindi. Learn these letters and then you are done."

I started to think I might get good enough to write a few sentences before Dadi left.

***

Megan came over that Sunday and I introduced her to Dadi and Montu. I was surprised that Megan was kind of shy with them. But she didn't seem shocked when Dadi gave her a hug. I think it was because I had told her to expect it.

"You're so lucky to have your grandma and cousin visit you for such a long time," she said.

"Last week, Montu and Kavita went outside to play every day after we got home from school. That's when I had to do my homework, so I didn't get a chance to join them. He was still jet-lagged, so he went to bed early. I didn't spend much time with him. But I have with Dadi. On Friday we cooked dessert."

"Really?" She seemed surprised. "Doesn't Kavita want to learn cooking too?"

I shook my head. "Ever since Kavita and Montu got into the back seat of the van on the way home from the airport, they have been best friends. It kind of bothers me. Montu is younger than me but older than Kavita. Smack in the middle. Shouldn't he be my friend too?"

"Hmmm . . ." Megan looked out the window.

"It's not fair that they have a bond."

"You have a bond with Dadi." She pointed outside. "Looks like they have a very sticky bond."

Montu and Kavita were at the picnic table. Whatever they were eating must have been sticky, because they were licking their fingers. Now I understood what Megan meant.

"I guess you just have to find something special to do

with Montu," she said. "An activity or a project that he really wants to do."

I thought about how I could entice Montu.

En-tice means to be tricky about making someone like you or what you're doing.

In-my-head list of ideas

* The two of us could do an art project.

* We could read a book together.

* Maybe Montu and I could play board games or cards.

* Montu wanted to spend time in our basement. Maybe there was something we could do in the basement that would be fun.

* Maybe we could set up a game room downstairs. We could take all the games down there.

Megan tapped my shoulder. "Stop making your list."

"What?"

"You must have been working on a list. Your frown is gone. What did you come up with?" Megan asked.

So I told her about my ideas.

"Sounds good. Now start reading." Megan added, "We need to work on our project. Don't overthink."

"Jay said the same thing." I sighed.

Megan and Jay were right. I should stop worrying. Sooner or later, I would get to spend some time with Montu.

## CHAPTER EIGHT

Maybe I shouldn't have worried about getting to spend time with Montu. Things changed during the next week. He wasn't as tired, so he stayed up as late as Kavita and I did.

As soon as I finished my homework on school days, Montu, Kavita, and I played outside. Most of the time Jay also came over. Sometimes all four of us walked over to our school playground with Dadi.

Just as I had planned, we set up a game room in the basement, with a card table, chairs, and our board games and puzzles. That meant we were prepared for a rainy day. Which was good, because it did rain on Wednesday. Instead of playing outside, we worked on a puzzle.

"This is the perfect place to hang out!" Montu said.

I had made him happy. I was being a good hostess.

On Friday evening Montu, Dad, Mom, Dadi, and I played cards. Kavita sat by us and drew pictures because she said cards were too difficult to figure out.

Everyone started talking in Hindi and I felt lost. "Can we talk in English?" I asked.

Dad shuffled the cards. "This is your chance to improve your Hindi, Nina."

Kavita gave me a look that said she knew how I felt.

I said, "It's hard to concentrate on the game and try to follow the conversation."

"Nina is right," Dadi said. "She is learning Hindi, but while we're playing, let's talk in English."

I smiled at her. She was being a kind guest.

＊＊＊

At breakfast on Saturday, I asked Dadi, "Would you like to come to our dance class today?"

She passed me a platter of mango slices. "Sure."

"Montu, will you come?" Kavita asked.

Dadi glanced at Montu. He shook his head just a tiny bit.

Sometimes Montu and Dadi signal each other. Like right now. She didn't ask if he wanted to come, and he didn't answer. She looked at him and he understood what she was asking. He shook his head and she knew what he meant. It's like they had an invisible link.

"What will you do when we are away?" Dadi asked.

He drank half of his milk before he answered. "I'll hang out with Jay."

Montu had never heard the phrase "hang out" until Kavita used it. Since then, he had found a reason to say it every single day. In the last day he had said it four times!

100

1 day = 24 hours

24 hours − 8 hours for sleeping = 16 hours

16 ÷ 4 = 4

That means he had used "hang out" every four hours while he was awake!

"Montu, you can't hang out with Jay." I served myself some mango. "He'll be with us. His mom teaches our class and she'll be driving all three of us there."

"Does he take class with you?" Montu asked.

"Sometimes he does," I said. "It depends on what kind of dance we're learning."

"Today it's bhangra," Kavita said.

Montu perked up. "Then I'd like to join you."

*Could Montu participate in our class?* I wondered.

> **Par-tic-i-pate** means to be able to take part in something.

I made an in-my-head list of reasons why he should be able to attend our class.

* Montu is already bored while we are at school.

* He would probably be even more bored while we were at dance class.

* He might enjoy going to dance class with us.

* I think if we asked Meera Masi if Montu could participate, she would say yes.

* On top of that, Jay would be there (he comes when there are specific dances that men do, like bhangra and a stick dance called raas). Montu would like that.

* On top of that, Montu is from India. He already seemed to be familiar with bhangra.

* He wanted to join us, so as his hostess, I should try to see if it was possible.

"Mom, should we ask Meera Masi if Montu can come to class?" I asked.

"Good idea," she said. "Let me give her a call."

After she hung up the phone, Mom said, "Meera Masi said yes. She will pick up all of you."

Just before we left, Montu whispered something to Mom. Then they both went upstairs.

"What did you want from my mom?" I asked when he came down.

Montu's eyes danced. "You'll find out soon enough."

✳✳✳

Before class began, Meera Masi introduced Dadi and Montu to everyone. We started with stretching exercises as we always do. I thought Montu would goof off, but Jay was serious and Montu watched and followed him.

I made an in-my-head list about why that might be.

* Maybe Dadi had said something to Montu before Meera Masi picked us up.
* Or maybe Montu was just following Jay. Or trying to impress everyone in the class.
* Maybe he really wanted to dance.
* Maybe he didn't want to be kicked out of the class.

Once we were done with stretching Meera Masi asked, "Ready to learn bhangra?"

Montu raised his hand.

Meera Masi said, "Yes, Montu?"

"I already know bhangra because my mom taught me. She is from Punjab, and bhangra comes from there," he said.

"You're right. It does come from the northwestern state of Punjab." Meera Masi added, "I'm glad you joined us."

I had no idea that Montu's mom and bhangra were from the same place. Nor did I know that Montu already knew bhangra, even though he is younger than me. I felt a tiny bit jealous. But not too much.

Meera Masi turned on the CD player. "Let's just listen to the music first."

The beat was fast and very lively. Without realizing, I started tapping my foot. Asha and Malini were doing the same thing.

As soon as the lyrics began, Montu started singing along. The song was in Punjabi, and I could make out a word here and there, but not many. Montu knew every single word of it *and* he seemed to understand what they meant. Montu knew Punjabi, Hindi, and English. That's three languages! He might even know more.

I thought I knew a lot of Hindi, but Montu knows more. He also knows Punjabi and I don't. And I am older than him. It was kind of overwhelming.

Over-whelm-ing means a situation that is hard to handle, so you feel like you're crushed under it. Like too much homework! Or too many languages!

But now I needed to pay attention. Meera Masi showed us how to move our hands, first up and then down, along with our feet. And of course, all of our movements had to go with the beat of the music. Right away Montu was dancing, humming along, and doing all kinds of moves while the rest of us were still trying to learn the first step.

I tried to ignore him, but it was difficult because he was so good. All I wanted to do was watch him. Everyone else did too.

I realized that I had stopped dancing. Soon, no one was moving except Montu.

"He's amazing," Malini said.

"Did you know Montu was such an awesome dancer?" Kavita asked.

I shook my head.

Meera Masi clapped her hands. "Stop watching Montu and focus on your own dancing. Let's start from the beginning." She motioned to all of us. "One, two, three, four . . ."

"This is too confusing," Kavita said. Her eyes were still on Montu.

"Don't look at him. Just do the first step," Asha said.

"But what he's doing looks like a lot more fun."

Meera Masi gave them a stern look and they started dancing again.

Kavita was right, though. It was fun to watch Montu, but trying to keep up with him was not going to work. His hands went up and then down, but then his leg went up and his arms went out to the sides. He clapped and then took a short scarf out of his pocket and waved it around as he danced.

That was what Montu wanted from Mom right before we left for the class! She gave him one of her scarves.

We all stood still again. Even Meera Masi was quiet.

When the music ended, Dadi cleared her throat. "Montu, it's time for you to rest for a while."

"I'm not tired. Why can't I dance?"

"You already did." She patted the chair next to her. "Come, Beta."

Montu sat down, looking grumpy. Dadi put her arm around him. I thought he would shrug her off, but he didn't.

"Montu, you dance beautifully," Meera Masi said. "Maybe you could take a break for a few minutes and then teach us some steps later?"

"Would you like to do that?" Dadi asked him.

"Yes." He smiled and leaned his head against her shoulder.

Meera Masi showed us three different steps. When we were finished learning them, she invited Montu to teach us one. Jay picked it up first.

Once everyone had mastered all four steps, we tried to put them together with the music. It wasn't easy and we kept making mistakes, except Montu, of course. But it was a lot of fun.

"Okay," Meera Masi said. "You all did a great job. I want to thank Montu for showing us a new step." She applauded and we joined in.

Montu beamed as if Meera Masi had served him a whole sweet pizza.

"Please practice these steps so next week we can successfully put them with the music and maybe learn a little more. I'll bring some scarves so we can dance with them," she said.

"Then we'll all be colorful like Montu!" Kavita said.

"Is it okay if I come again?" Montu asked Meera Masi. "Please?" He was so polite and respectful that even a mean person would have said yes. And Meera Masi is sweet and kind.

"Of course, Montu," she said. "We would all love for you to join us."

✳✳✳

On the drive home, Montu said, "You are a fast learner, Jay."

"Thanks," Jay said. "Like my mom, I love to dance."

"He can also break-dance," Kavita added.

"What?" Montu almost slid off the seat. "I always wanted to learn that. Can you teach me, Jay?"

"Sure." Jay asked, "Mom, when can Montu come over?"

"Next Sunday?" She glanced sideways at Dadi. "If that's okay with you."

Montu tapped Dadi's seat. "Dadi, may I? Please, may I hang out with Jay?"

"Yes," Dadi said. "Kavita has a birthday party to attend, and Nina and I will work on Hindi."

"Thank you!" Montu said in his outside voice.

Montu and Jay seemed happy about that.

I was not. What was bothering me?

I made an in-my-head list about why I was unhappy.

* Kavita and Montu were already good friends.
* They spend time together.
* Now Montu wants to learn break dancing from Jay.
* Jay said he would teach him.
* That means they will spend time together.
* That mean they will be good friends.
* I play with Montu too, but always also with Kavita and sometimes even Jay. Or Mom, Dad, and Dadi. Never just Montu and me alone.

✳ | Will I ever get to be friends with Montu the way Kavita and Jay are?

I was restless.

> **Rest-less** means you can't find any calm and peace.

That wasn't something I wanted to be. A restless person can't do their job well. I needed to calm down so I could be a perfect hostess.

Maybe I was thinking too much about myself. Was I being selfish and un-hostess-like?

# CHAPTER NINE

On Sunday we drove to Wisconsin Dells and took a boat ride. The tour guide pointed to some rock formations ahead. "This sandstone was carved by glacial water, even though glaciers never reached this part of the state."

"What are glaciers?" Montu whispered.

It was my duty as a hostess to explain. "A glacier is a huge mass of ice formed by snow, rocks, and debris. It moves very slowly and shapes the landscape around it. Many parts of Wisconsin were covered with it, including Madison."

"I didn't see any glaciers in Madison," Montu said. "Everything is green there."

"The glaciers melted away a long, long time ago."

After our tour, we drove to Mirror Lake State Park for a picnic. While the adults set up, the kids walked around the lake, shimmering under a blue sky.

Montu said, "The glaciers sound amazing. I want to learn more about them."

I picked up a pebble. "Maybe when Kavita and I are in school you can do some research."

"I will," he said. "Or I could ask Mr. or Mrs. Crump."

"What? Have you talked to them more?"

"Of course. I've been helping them out."

I could feel my eyes widen in surprise. "With what?"

"I carried the bricks when Mr. Crump made the patio in the back. And when that was done, your mom and I planted hydrangeas around it."

I turned the pebble between my fingers as I made a quick list in my head.

✳ Montu had a lot of free time while Kavita and I were in school.

* I had never asked what he did while we were gone after that first day.

* I assumed he read, ate, napped, and got bored.

* Or waited and waited for us all day long.

* As a good hostess, when we returned from school I should have asked what he did while we were gone. Every single day.

"Why are you quiet?" Montu asked.

"I . . . I didn't realize you were so busy."

"I had to do something. I couldn't hang out with you, so I found someone else."

"Children," Dad called. "Come over here."

We walked back to them.

"Let's sit by the shore here," Dad said.

I pointed at a trail marker. "Aren't we going on a hike?"

Dad is always ready to go for a walk, but today he seemed reluctant.

**Re-luc-tant** means to not be sure about something and hold back. It's like if you have your favorite treat and someone wants it, you might be reluctant to give it to them.

"I . . . I don't think that's a good idea," he said.

"Why not?" I asked.

He leaned closer and spoke quietly. "Dadi is tired. Why don't we have a snack? Then Mom and I will sit here with her while you, Kavita, and Montu run around."

I realized that today I had been a careless hostess to one of my guests. I hadn't noticed that Dadi looked tired.

Mom and Dad spread a couple of blankets on the ground, and we ate popcorn and drank lemonade we had brought from home.

While the grown-ups talked, the three of us kids played hide-and-seek. Kavita and Montu hid while I counted to ten in Hindi. "Ready or not, here I come," I said when I was done.

Our picnic area was surrounded by trees. I looked

behind each of them for Montu and Kavita, but I didn't see them. "Found you!" I shouted when I spied Montu behind a rock.

"It would be more fun if we didn't have to stay so close." He pointed at a bigger rock in the distance. "I'd have gone over there."

Kavita peeked out from behind a tree trunk. "The rule is that we can't go farther than that clump of trees. And we have to follow that rule."

"I know. You two never break rules."

"Why, do you?" I asked.

He shrugged.

✳✳✳

We drove back home, showered, and went to our favorite Indian restaurant for dinner.

When we sat down at the table, Dad asked, "Montu, how would you like to visit a school here?"

"It's his vacation!" Kavita gasped. "He doesn't want to go to school. He wants to play."

"I know, Kavita." Dad put his hand on her arm. "But it might be an interesting experience for him."

Montu's eyes were wide. "Can I do that?"

I wasn't quite sure if I wanted Montu to come to school with me and Kavita. He had been the best one in our dance class. He had helped the Crumps and he and Jay had made plans together. What would he do at school with us? Be a star student? Become the most popular kid? He might make so many new friends that he would have even less time for me.

Was it even fair for Dad to ask Montu if he wanted to go to school without asking Kavita and me first?

Maybe my principal or our teachers would say that Montu couldn't come.

*But why is Montu so eager to come to my school?* I wondered as I ate my dal soup.

I made a quick in-my-head list of possible explanations.

* Montu is on vacation.

* He is far away from his friends, who are also out of school.

* All day he is home alone with Dadi while we're in school and Mom and Dad are working.

* When he first got here, he was tired and jet-lagged. But he isn't anymore.

* Other than Dadi and sometimes the Crumps, he has no other company.

* It must be boring for him to wait all day for us (mostly Kavita) to return.

* He has never been to school here. He doesn't know what it's like.

* He might like to meet some other kids.

* If Montu only came for a day, he wouldn't have time to become friends with any of them.

* But it would still be exciting for him. It would be something new for him to do.
* Maybe it was a good idea.

"Montu is on a visitor visa, so he can't attend school here," Mom said. "I already checked."

"What's a visitor visa?" Kavita asked.

"When someone travels from one country to another, they need to ask permission to enter," she said. "Since Montu and Dadi came from India to the USA, they had to apply for a visa."

Dad shook his head. "I think he should be able to *visit* Nina's and Kavita's classes. He's not attending school."

"You might be right," Mom said.

"Then he won't have to do any homework, will he?" Kavita asked.

"No," Dad replied.

"Then I want him to come," she said. "I want Montu to meet my teacher and my friends. I want him to see my classroom and the gym. And I want the whole school to see my newest friend from India."

"He's your only friend from India," I reminded Kavita.

"I know, but 'newest' sounds better, Nina." She asked, "Mom, will you find out if he can come?"

"Please," Montu pleaded. "I'd like to go to an American school. Even just for one class."

"I will," she replied.

"Let's continue to enjoy this dinner now," Dadi said. "Please pass the eggplant and potatoes, Nina."

Now I couldn't wait for Montu to come to school. As a perfect hostess I would do my best to show him a good time. Montu was excited to visit our school, so I should let him see my classroom, the gym, and the lunchroom, meet my friends and teachers, and see how we learn in a real American school.

**✳✳✳**

The next morning, I woke up just as the sun was rising. I saw a light on downstairs. Sometimes Mom gets up early to work or Dad goes for a run. Maybe one of them was already up. I went downstairs and found Dadi making tea.

"I hope you slept well, Beta," she said.

I nodded. "I'm hungry."

"I just finished my yoga and meditation, so we can have breakfast together."

I took out a bowl for my cereal. "Why do you meditate every morning? What does it do?"

Dadi added some cinnamon to the boiling water. "It helps me reflect and calm my mind."

I had felt restless when Montu asked Jay if he could teach him to break-dance. It had made my mind kind of choppy. I also had a difficult time learning to write Hindi because different thoughts kept popping up in my brain. I asked Dadi, "Do you think meditation would help my mind calm down?"

"It might help quiet the thoughts and ideas running all over your brain, Beta."

How did Dadi know about my brain with all its different idea tracks? I made a quick in-my-head list.

- ✳ Maybe Mom or Dad told Dadi how I have too many tracks in my brain.
- ✳ Maybe Dadi noticed on her own that I have too many thoughts.
- ✳ Maybe she knows about it because she saw I had a hard time paying attention when she was teaching me Hindi.
- ✳ Or maybe she has too many thoughts, just like I do.

Dadi sat at the table with me. She had her chai and I had cereal and milk.

When we had finished, she said, "Close your eyes. Take a deep breath. As you take in the air, imagine that your lungs are getting full and then slowly let the air go out."

I breathed like she had said. Slow and steady, in and out, in and out.

It felt good.

"Now keep breathing deeply, in and out," Dadi said. "But keep your eyes closed and think of something that makes you happy."

"A jasmine? Can I think about a flower?" I asked.

"Yes, you can meditate on a flower."

"What does 'meditate on a flower' mean?"

"That means to still your mind and focus on a thing that makes you happy—like a flower."

I closed my eyes and thought of a jasmine blossom. I could picture its moon-white color, and almost smell its sweet scent. But then I wondered. Should I have picked a rose to mediate on? What about tulips? They're blooming now. I should have picked lilac. Yes, I can smell them now. What about all the colorful leaves of fall? I love them. Why not them?

Could I switch from a flower to leaves?

Maybe I could meditate on leaves in the fall.

"Are you focusing on jasmine?" Dadi asked.

I opened my eyes. "I was but then my mind wandered off. How could you tell?"

"Your eyelids fluttered and then your fingers began to twitch," she said. "Your breathing got uneven too."

"Why does that matter?" I asked.

"When you concentrate on your breath, it is smooth and even. When you lose concentration, the other thoughts darting around your mind make your breathing uneven."

I sighed. "Meditation is hard."

"Yes, the mind is like a monkey with a ladder."

"I've never heard of that."

She smiled. "If you give a monkey a ladder it will not sit calmly. It will climb up, hang from a rung, jump down, and whatnot. Our mind does the same. It hops from one idea to another and plays all kinds of tricks. It is difficult to calm it."

"What you call a ladder is what I call tracks, Dadi," I said. Then I explained to her how my brain has so many tracks and jumps from one to another.

"I see." She rested her palms on my shoulders. Her touch felt as soft as flower petals. "I'll help you. It is not easy, but with practice, you could make your mind stop jumping tracks."

We started again.

"Breathe in and out, in and out," she said.

I did.

"Now think of a jasmine. Its lush green leaves and its moon-white flowers. Its delicate petals and sweet smell."

I did.

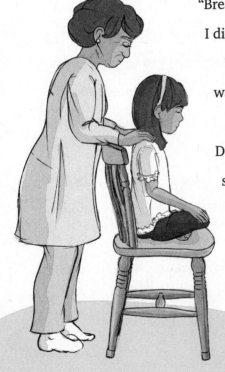

"Breathe in and out," Dadi said.

I did.

Then somewhere along the way, I lost the image. Again.

My mind wandered away. Do jasmine and lilac smell the same, or is there a difference? Do I like one better than the other? Maybe combining them would make the best-smelling scent. I bet perfume makers use scents from many flowers.

I opened my eyes again without realizing it.

"Focus please," Dadi said. "It will become easier. You need practice to master your mind."

I nodded even though I didn't know if I could ever master my mind.

But did I even need to?

Would I recognize my mind if it turned calm and peaceful? Would my brain feel empty if all the idea tracks went missing?

Maybe keeping lists was enough for me and my mind.

I shook my head to get rid of my scattering thoughts.

Dadi glanced at the clock. "You better get ready for school."

## CHAPTER TEN

I had been trying to be a perfect hostess for three weeks. That meant it was only three more weeks until Dadi and Montu would leave. We were halfway through their visit. I couldn't believe it! I was just starting to get used to having them here every day.

When I got home from school on Friday, I went straight to Kavita's room. I picked up Lucky and opened Sakhi. I sat on the bed and started to make a list of how their visit was going so far.

* I like having Dadi and Montu here because our house doesn't seem as boring as before.

* Usually, Mom is busiest with work in the spring and doesn't have much time to cook.

* Dad's cooking is good, but he makes the same dishes. It gets tiring.

* Dad is happy too, because he gets to eat all his favorite dishes made by his mom just like the ones he grew up eating. (Although some of them are not that great. Like gooey drumstick vegetable!)

* Montu and Kavita spend a lot of time together. I still can't tell if I like that or not.

* Sometimes I like it because then I can spend time with Dadi.

* Most of the time I like Montu, but sometimes he can be annoying.

* Is it bad to not always like a member of your family—or to not always like your guest?
* I still don't know if Dadi and Montu are family or guests.
* I still don't know if I am a perfect hostess, but I think I am starting to be a good one.

As much as I loved having Dadi and Montu visit, I missed not having my own room. I liked being with everyone most of the time. But sometimes I wanted to be by myself. In my room. Just Sakhi, Lucky, and me. Like right now.

But I wasn't alone for long. Just as I closed Sakhi, Montu came in.

"Where is Kavita?" I asked.

"Dadi is teaching her how to braid her hair." He looked lost. "Can I hang out with you?"

"Your favorite new expression is 'hang out,'" I said. "Anyway, you mostly hang out with Kavita. You don't spend that much time with me."

"You have homework, and she doesn't. And by the time you're done with it we are already playing something." He added with a smile, "So how can I hang out with you as much as I do with Kavita?"

He was right. Even with Montu and Dadi visiting I still followed my routine.

Rou-tine means something that you do in order. My weekday routine is come home, eat snack, and do homework.

When Kavita and Montu sit together in the back seat of the van they immediately start talking, laughing, and giggling. That's their routine. Then I remembered that I didn't want to sit in the back seat with them; I wanted to be with Dadi. I realized that Montu and Kavita hadn't shut me out on purpose.

"You're right, Montu," I said. "I have a lot more home-work than Kavita does."

Kavita rushed into the room. "How do you like my hair?" She twirled to show off her braid.

"First class," Montu said.

I said, "It makes you look older."

"Nina," she said, "if you braid your hair, we will look like twins."

"Not a chance," Montu said. "Nina is so much taller than you."

Kavita stood by me. "But if we had the same hairstyle, I would look like her sister."

"You already are my sister, and we look alike," I said.

"You're right," she said. "What were you two doing while I was with Dadi?"

"Talking," he said.

"Just for a little while." I added, "Before that I was spending time with Sakhi."

Montu looked around. "Who is Sakhi?"

Kavita has known Sakhi ever since I have had Sakhi. She knows I share a lot of things in Sakhi and that I make lists. But I realized I had never told Montu about Sakhi.

"That's Nina's notebook. The one she's holding," Kavita said. "'Sakhi' means 'friend' in Hindi."

"I know what sakhi means," he said.

"Of course you do," Kavita said. "You're a master of Hindi."

"I'm not."

"You sure are."

He shook his head. "Na, na, na."

"Accha, accha, accha," Kavita said in the same tone.

"Na and accha, be quiet," I said.

A big mistake.

Now Montu's attention was back on me. He was staring at Sakhi. Would he want to read it? Would he ask? If he did, I'd have to say no to him. A perfect hostess wouldn't do that to her guest, would she?

All these thoughts made me feel desperate.

**Des-per-ate** means you're in real trouble and could use some help.

Kavita pulled at Montu's hand. "Let's finish that hundred-piece penguin puzzle," she said.

"Now?" Montu asked.

"Well," Kavita said, "if you want to finish it before dinner, we'd better do it now."

He pointed out the window. "The sun is still shining. It's not dinnertime for hours!"

"It's already six," I said.

He scratched his head. "I forget how long the days are here. It stays light so much later than it does in India. I wish we had such long days at home."

"If you had long days in the summer," I pointed out, "then you would have much shorter days in the winter."

"I wouldn't want that," Montu said. "In December there are two fewer hours of daylight than in June, and I don't like it."

"If you want to finish that puzzle," Kavita said, jabbing him with her finger, "no more dillydallying."

"Accha, I'm coming," he said.

Kavita glanced over her shoulder as they left the room. I joined my palms and bent down. "Thank you," I mouthed.

I put Sakhi on the dresser. Maybe Montu had been interested in Sakhi at first, but Kavita changed the track in his brain to the penguin puzzle. She had sidetracked him.

---

**Side-track** means to put something to the side, on another track.

---

Should I just assume he had forgotten?

Ugh, sometimes I wish I was as direct as Kavita. I could have told Montu right away that I didn't want him to read Sakhi. That it was my notebook and it was private. Maybe that would have been better. He is curious. But he hadn't asked to see Sakhi. Maybe I was assuming he was interested in it, but he wasn't.

But if I told him now not to read Sakhi, I might bring his attention right back to it. The only thing I could do to keep him from reading Sakhi was to keep it safe with me. All the time. I put Sakhi in my backpack.

But I still didn't feel reassured.

Re-as-sured means to feel sure and have no worries.

In-my-head list of why I wasn't reassured

* Now I would have to carry my backpack with Sakhi in it even when I was home.

* I would have to take my backpack in the bathroom with me when I showered, keep it under my chair when I ate, and have it next to me in bed when I slept. (No one could shower, eat, or sleep while wearing a backpack.)

* I would have to take Sakhi to school.

* I could lose Sakhi at school and never get it back. Sakhi would be gone forever.

* What if someone at school read Sakhi?

* What if they made fun of what I've written in Sakhi?

✳ What if they shared my personal thoughts

with the whole class? Or the whole school?

Or the whole world?

I took Sakhi out of my backpack.

Dadi peeked in. "Ready to come down for dinner?"

I nodded.

She asked, "What's the trouble?"

I told her about Sakhi and what happened with Montu. "Do you think he will sneak a look at it?"

She came in and sat on the bed. "Why do you think he would do that?"

"I think sometimes he breaks rules. He kind of admitted to it when we played hide-and-seek at Mirror Lake."

"I guess he does." She looked thoughtful. "Most likely he will be busy playing and having fun. He probably will forget about Sakhi."

I sat down by her. "What if he does not?"

"Would you like me to talk to Montu?"

I shook my head. "No, he hasn't even asked me to show it to him."

"You are experiencing pain before a fall."

I kind of understood what she meant. I was worrying about something that might not happen. "I think I'll just keep my notebook with me."

"You're a planner with too many ideas," she said. "You give a lot of thought to each of them. You devote your energy to them. Am I right?"

I remembered the perfect hostess list I had made before Dadi and Montu had even arrived. "Yes."

Dadi smiled. "When your imagination takes over, it can bring worries. Like now." She stroked my back. "Let go a little, Nina. I don't think Montu would snoop. He is just happy to be doing whatever he's doing."

That sounded like Kavita to me too. Maybe Montu and Kavita were alike, and that's why they enjoyed spending so much time together.

"Come." Dadi got up. "Let's not keep everyone waiting."

## CHAPTER ELEVEN

Dad, Montu, and Dadi left for Chicago before we returned home from school on Monday. After that, they were going to drive to Milwaukee and then to Door County before coming home on Saturday. I wished we all could have gone, but Mom was busy with her work, and Kavita and I had to go to school.

Our house felt empty. It didn't seem right that Montu wasn't waiting in our front yard to greet us after school. I missed Dadi's cooking, our talks, and our lessons.

After school, Kavita drew and colored while I did my

homework. When I was done, we walked over to Jay's house and played outside.

I kept working on Hindi while Dadi was gone because I didn't want to forget what I had already learned. It also gave me something to do. I opened a book and tried to read some of the simple Hindi phrases. I was surprised that I was able to understand some of them. When I wasn't sure if I had figured something out, I went to Mom for help.

"Does this say 'aap kahaan ja rahen hain'?" I asked. "'Where are you going?'"

"Yes," she said. "Nina, you have learned a lot in such a short time."

"After Dadi goes back to India, could you keep teaching me? I don't want to forget."

"Certainly."

"Mom, when Dadi and Montu came, I thought I would teach them everything. I didn't realize I would learn so much from them."

"What else have you learned from them?" she asked.

"Montu showed our dance class bhangra steps. He's an expert card player. Dadi taught me Hindi, how to make gajar halwa, and how to meditate. Now every morning I meditate on a jasmine flower."

Mom's eyebrows went up. "Why a jasmine flower?"

"Why not?"

She smiled. "Are you enjoying their visit?"

"I am. Even though it's hard not to have my own room, I'm glad they're here."

"You have been very mature about it and I'm proud of you." Mom picked up her pencil. "By the way, Montu has permission to visit your school."

"Accha!"

I went back to work on my Hindi. I felt very calm. Maybe that jasmine meditation helped me calm my mind. I wasn't sure.

"It's not the same without Montu and Dadi," I said to Kavita when we were in bed.

*"Our family has shrunk, like a balloon without air. But it's okay, Montu will be back,"* Kavita sang.

"They'll only be here for two more weeks. Then they return to India," I sighed.

Kavita's face fell.

"Don't worry, I'll always be here," I said.

"Yes, Ninai," she whispered.

✱✱✱

Kavita was at her friend Avery's house when Dadi, Montu, and Dad returned from their trip. This was my chance to spend time with Montu.

"We missed you at our dance class," I said as we sat on a picnic bench enjoying popsicles.

"I wish we could have all gone on this trip. It would have been so much more fun."

"Did you like Chicago, Milwaukee, or Door County the best?" I asked.

"I like Lake Michigan the best. I couldn't believe it was

the same lake in all those three places," Montu said. "It reminds me of the Arabian Sea."

"Is there any other place you would like to visit?"

"I only have two weeks left, so I want to hang out with you and Kavita. I want to visit your school, though."

"Of course!"

He beamed.

✻✻✻

Kavita, Jay, Montu, and I walked to school together on Monday. Mom had arranged for Montu to visit my class first and then go to Kavita's. Mom was going to pick him up before lunch and take him home.

I realized that I had no idea what Montu's school was like. I wondered if it was different from ours. I was curious about his classes, his homework, his teachers, and his friends.

I made an in-my-head list of my questions.

* What time does Montu go to school?

* When does he come home?

* What is his favorite subject?

* Is his school large or small?

* How many students are in his class?

* Does he bring lunch or is there a cafeteria?

* What does he do at recess? Does he have recess?

"Do you walk to school?" I asked him.

"No way," he said. "It is far, and my backpack is too heavy. I go by school bus. Do you walk even when it is snowing?"

"Yup."

"We only get a ride if it is raining," Kavita said.

"But isn't it very cold when it snows?"

"Sometimes it's freezing cold, and you can even see your breath," I said. "You just have to bundle up."

"Luckily, it's not that far," Jay added.

"You don't have to wear a uniform like we do."

I had never seen Montu in his school uniform. I didn't even realize he wore one. Maybe someday I could go to India and attend his class. Maybe I could tell them about the USA, just like he was going to talk to our classes about India.

Kavita sang, *"It's boring, like snoring, to wear the same clothing every single morning!"*

✳✳✳

As soon as Montu and I got to my classroom he said, "It is so colorful! Everyone is wearing different clothes and you have posters, books, and even plants. I could hang out here all day!"

He snapped a picture with his camera.

I pointed at a desk next to mine. "Look!" It had a place-holder sign that read "Welcome, Montu!"

"Wow!" He took another picture then sat down.

Ms. Lapin walked in and Montu whispered, "Don't you stand up when your teacher comes?"

"No," I whispered.

"Today we have a special guest," Ms. Lapin said.

Montu's face turned red. I think he was happy but also a little nervous.

She asked, "Nina, would you like to introduce him?"

Montu and I stood in front of the class. "This is my cousin Manan, but everyone calls him Montu. He lives in India and has come here for a visit. He is ready to answer all your questions," I said.

Then I sat back down.

Many hands shot up.

Ms. Lapin pointed to Kyle.

"Have you seen the Taj Mahal?"

"Yes," Montu said. "But I was only four, so I don't remember much."

Tyler asked the next question. "Nina told us about Holi. Do you really color each other?"

Montu gave the biggest smile I have ever seen. "Yes. It

comes in March. We spray each other with water guns and use pink powder called gulal."

"What about your clothes?" Emma asked. "Don't they get ruined?"

"We always wear old clothes," Montu replied, "the ones we don't want to keep, because they do get stained."

"Is that your favorite holiday?" Jay wanted to know.

Montu's face scrunched up. "I think my favorite one is called Makar Sankrant, a holiday where we fly kites."

"There's a holiday for kite flying?" someone asked.

"Yes. It is celebrated in January in honor of the Sun God. We also donate to poor people, and we get to eat sweets made out of sesame seeds and brown sugar."

Emma looked shocked. "You fly kites in the snow?"

"We don't have snow in January in India. The weather is usually perfect. My dad and I fly about forty kites that day."

I thought Montu was exaggerating.

Ex-ag-ger-at-ing means telling tall tales.

I didn't want him to get away with that. "Are you sure it's forty kites and not four?" I asked.

"Forty," he said. "I can certainly count."

Kyle said, "That can't be true. Why would you need so many? I've had the same kite for the last two years."

"Same kite for two years?" Now Montu looked like he thought Kyle was telling tall tales. "I do fly forty or so. It's because we have kite fights. When someone cuts off your kite you lose it."

"Someone cuts your kite string with a pair of scissors?" Kyle asked. "Why would they do that?"

"No." Montu put his two index fingers up. "Imagine these are strings attached to two kites that are flying." Then he crossed them. "As they go back and forth"—he rubbed his fingers against each other—"one of them is going to break. That kite will come tumbling down."

"Awesome," Kyle said without raising his hand. "I want to fight kites!"

Ms. Lapin gave him a look.

"I can show you," Montu said. "I have a video."

Kyle's hand went up.

"No more kite questions," Ms. Lapin said.

He lowered his hand.

Montu answered questions about traveling in India, and food, and even Bollywood films.

Then Tyler said, "Nina says she knows Hindi. Do you know it too?"

"Yes," Montu said.

"How about Spanish?" someone else asked.

"No. Besides English I only know Indian languages."

"How many?" Kyle asked.

Ms. Lapin had to remind Kyle again to raise his hand.

Montu held up four fingers. "Hindi, Punjabi, Marathi, and Gujarati."

"And English! That's five," Ms. Lapin said. "That's quite an achievement!"

"All my friends know many languages," Montu said. "Some know a lot more than I do."

"One last question," Ms. Lapin said.

Jay raised his hand and Ms. Lapin called on him.

"What do you like the best about your visit?" he asked.

I remembered how Montu had asked all of us to pick

one thing we had liked the most at the Olbrich Gardens. Then I had asked him if he liked Chicago, Milwaukee, or Door County best. I wondered how Montu felt being asked the same questions he had asked us.

Montu thought for a minute. "Everything. I like everything here."

Jay glanced at me and smiled.

Ms. Lapin said, "Maybe you can tell us a few things you like in this country."

"I like that I have cousins here to play with," Montu said. "I like strawberries and blackberries and all the other berries you have here. I like the scent of lilac. I like that you don't have to wear a uniform to school or carry too many books. I like that you have very few students in your class. On a rainy day I like to play in a basement."

"That's a lot of things." Ms. Lapin smiled. "You do like everything here."

He nodded. Not a Montu-nod, an up-and-down one.

"Thank you for sharing," Ms. Lapin said. "Let's give Montu a round of applause."

We all did. Then he sat down next to me.

"OK, we will start the class with a math quiz on percentages," Ms. Lapin said.

She handed out copies of the quiz. Montu extended his hand, and she gave him one too.

"Ten minutes," Ms. Lapin said.

Montu gave her his quiz back in less than five minutes.

Jay glanced at me. "Too hard for him?"

"Probably," I whispered back.

Montu was smiling, though. Did he finish it? No way. How could he have?

When we were done, Ms. Lapin said, "Good job, Montu. You got all of them right."

I almost fell off my chair. How could Montu know five languages, be a kite fighter, and do math so fast when he's younger than I am? He was a genius.

> **Ge-nius** means someone who is super-smart. Like Montu.

"They were easy," Montu said.

I already knew Montu worked fast. He didn't need to also say that it was easy.

Montu was probably good—okay, excellent—at math. But he didn't have to take the quiz. He could have kept his smartness all inside his brain. I was not happy with his flaunting his math skills.

> **Flaunt-ing** means showing off.

When we started doing geography, I kept my eye on Montu. Ms. Lapin asked, "Who can tell me what an archipelago is?" She wrote the word on the whiteboard, breaking it into syllables.

*Ar-chi-pel-a-go*

I expected Montu to know the answer, but he whispered to me, "Is that a real word?"

I nodded. So Montu didn't know everything. He didn't know about archipelagoes and he hadn't known about glaciers either.

I raised my hand, but Ms. Lapin called on Emma.

"An archipelago is a group of islands," she answered.

"Very good," Ms. Lapin said.

When geography was over, Montu went to Kavita's classroom.

At recess everyone told me that they thought Montu was smart and nice. I guessed they didn't think he was flaunting.

# CHAPTER TWELVE

Montu was waiting for us when we got home. "Did you like our school?" I asked him.

He gave his Montu-nod. "It was good. I like your teacher very much. Is she always so nice?"

Mom had left a big bowl of popcorn on the kitchen counter, and it smelled delicious.

"Yes." I washed and dried my hands. "I think Ms. Lapin is the best teacher in school."

"No way," Kavita said. "Mrs. Jabs is. Montu, why didn't you like her?"

Montu put his hands up. "I never said I didn't like her. She's also very nice."

Kavita took a handful of popcorn. "Montu, who do you like the best, Mrs. Jabs or Ms. Lapin?"

"Kavita," Montu asked, "do I have to pick one?"

She nodded.

"When it is about two people and you choose one over the other, you can hurt someone's feelings," he said.

"But we're not telling them," Kavita said.

Soon, one or both of them would ask me to take a side or get upset. I took a handful of popcorn and slipped out of the kitchen. Kavita and Montu were so busy arguing that they didn't even notice.

Why did Montu like to play with Kavita when she challenged him all the time? I made an in-my-head list of possible explanations.

* Montu doesn't have brothers or sisters.

* That means no one ever challenges him.

✱ No one argues or fights with him.

✱ No one asks him to share things.

✱ I try to be a perfect hostess, so I don't challenge, argue, fight, or ask him to share with me.

✱ Only Kavita does that.

✱ Maybe he likes that because it is new to him.

✱ Maybe he thinks it is fun to argue.

Could I become more like Kavita and also be a perfect hostess? Which was more important?

Maybe Dadi could help me understand Montu.

I found her in her room—I mean *my* room. I mean my room that I had given up for her and Montu.

Dadi closed her book and glanced up. "Where are Kavita and Montu?"

"Eating popcorn and arguing," I said. "I snuck away."

"I see," she said. "You didn't want to be a tree crushed by two bulls."

I was confused. "What does that mean?"

"That is a saying," Dadi said. "When two bulls fight, a tree standing quietly between them can be damaged."

I thought for a moment. "You mean when two bull-headed people argue, the innocent person watching them can get hurt?"

"Exactly."

I imagined Kavita and Montu as two bulls and me in the middle as a tree. I smiled.

"What is it?" Dadi asked.

"I was just imagining them like real bulls and . . ." I started to laugh.

"And you as a tree?"

I nodded.

She laughed too. Then she asked, "What did you think of Montu's school visit, Nina?"

"It went well. All my classmates and my teacher liked him a lot."

"He must have behaved."

"He did," I said. "Montu is so good at math. How could he know more than I do when he's younger?"

"Most of the schools in India are very demanding and competitive. He attends one of the top schools, so he has to work hard. But he also gets in trouble for not following the rules." Dadi put her book away. "Montu said he liked your school a lot better than his own."

"My school isn't so strict and my teacher is very kind. She makes learning enjoyable. Like today our class learned about India from Montu in a fun way. Maybe Montu liked the way she teaches and he behaved well because he wanted to. Not because anyone was making him."

She was quiet before saying, "Accha nirikshan kiya."

"What does that mean?" I asked.

"It means that you made a good observation."

I felt happy and warm inside.

It was Friday. There was only a week before Montu and Dadi were going to leave. When Kavita and I got home from school, Montu looked super-excited. I supposed he couldn't wait to spend the weekend with us—the last full weekend of their stay.

"Hey," he said, running toward us. "I have been waiting to have a snack with you like forever." He had picked up "like forever" recently, though I didn't know from whom.

Mom called to me from the front stoop. "I've got one phone call to make, Nina. Could you please get some snacks for everyone?"

"Yes," I said. "I'll see what we have in the refrigerator."

Dadi and Montu always try new foods at least once. Since they had arrived, we had learned that Montu likes creamy peanut butter and Dadi likes crunchy. They both like hummus and neither care for mushrooms. Dadi loves blueberries the most, and Montu's favorite is strawberries.

I went into the kitchen, washed my hands, and rummaged through the refrigerator for something yummy to eat.

> **Rum-mage** means to look around or search.

There was a lot of stuff in there, but I only took out a few things.

* Two apples
* Two pears
* A bag of walnuts
* A container of hummus
* A wedge of Gouda cheese

"Can I help you, Nina?" Dadi came into the kitchen.

"Yes, please," I said as I washed the pears and apples.

"I will cut the fruits, if you share with me," she said.

"Sure. For your help, I'll pay you in slices." I took out one more apple and a pear and washed them too.

She cut the fruit while I got four plates.

"What's that?" She pointed at the cheese.

"It's Gouda cheese. Want to try some?"

"Sure."

I gave her a cheese knife. "Cut it with this one."

I opened the door and called out, "Kavita and Montu, come in if you want to eat." Then I got some bowls and a spoon for the hummus.

"Did you try the Gouda?" I asked Dadi.

There was something in her mouth, but she wasn't chewing. Instead, she had a funny look on her face.

I picked up another piece of cheese and peeled off the red wax. Then I plopped it in my mouth.

She covered her mouth. "Why did you take that off?"

"The wax?" I asked. "Oh no! Did you eat that as well as the cheese?"

She nodded. I handed her a napkin so she could spit it out. Then she rinsed her mouth. She said something.

"Sorry, I didn't understand you," I said.

"I said in Sanskrit, 'I got a fly in my first bite.' It is an old saying."

"Oh!" I gave her another piece of cheese, this time without the wax. "No flies, I promise."

"Much better," she said after she finished chewing. "You must think I am such a fool, Nina."

I shook my head. "Of course I don't."

"We won't tell anyone, accha?" she asked.

I covered my mouth with a piece of wax. "My lips are sealed."

Then we burst out laughing.

"What's so funny?" Montu asked as he and Kavita came in.

I scooped hummus into my bowl while they washed their hands. "Oh, this and that and stuff," I said.

Kavita's eyes narrowed. "What's that supposed to mean?" She knew Dadi and I were hiding something.

"Kavita," I said, "you and Montu laugh a lot, don't you?"

"I guess." She sat down and picked up a pear slice.

"But you don't always share with us why you laugh, right?"

"It's because we're silly," Montu said. "And it's hard to explain silly stuff."

"Exactly," I said. "Dadi and I are the same way."

"Not Dadi," Montu said. "She never laughs like that in India."

I dipped my apple slice in hummus. "Montu, everyone has a silly partner. Yours is Kavita and mine is Dadi."

Kavita sang, *"We all need a partner, one that is silly and smart, giggly and grand."*

"Not again," Montu said. "Why do you always have to sing?"

"Why do you always have to ask why I have to sing?" Kavita lifted her chin. "You should know the answer by now. Shouldn't you?"

"I guess," Montu said. "But I don't."

Dadi pushed her chair back. "Who wants to help me make okra?"

"Not me," said Kavita.

"Not me," said Montu.

"I do," I said.

Kavita and Montu left, and Dadi took the okra out of the refrigerator. "Remember to wash and dry them before you cut," she said.

I washed them in a colander and let the water drain out.

I dried each pod with a clean kitchen towel, then handed them to her to cut. "Why do we have to dry them?" I asked.

"If okra and water mix it gets slimy," she said. "I like my okra crispy."

"I do too." I asked, "Is what Montu said true? You never laugh like that in India?"

Dadi picked up another pod and began slicing. "It's because I don't have a silly partner there."

"I just made that up! You don't really think it's true that everyone has a silly partner, do you?"

"It is true. Montu also doesn't laugh like this at home."

"Maybe he has a silly partner at school?"

"I think the whole class is his partner. He makes all of them laugh."

"Montu, the class clown?"

She took out a pan. "That's him. Pour some oil in here, please."

I opened the drawer to take out a measuring spoon.

"Na, na," she said. "No need to measure. Just guess."

I did. I must have put in the right amount, because she didn't correct me.

"Now add some cumin seeds."

This time I didn't go looking for a teaspoon. I added what looked like the right amount.

"Perfect," she said. "Now, the key to crispy okra is not to cover them while they cook."

"Is that because putting the lid on would produce steam? And we don't want steam because steam is water, right? That would make slimy okra."

"Exactly."

While the okra cooked, Dadi said, "Let's make roti dough. Get the flour, please."

I dumped some flour in a bowl. "Is this enough?"

"A little more," she said. "Then add about a teaspoon of oil and mix it together."

"That part is easy," I said.

"Now add water and keep mixing."

"How much water? A cup, or more than that?"

She shook her head. "I never measure it."

Now I was worried. What if I added too much? I filled a glass with water and put a little in, and then a tiny bit more, one dribble at a time.

"When you first start out you can afford to put in a generous amount," Dadi said. "Then you have to be careful to make your dough the right consistency."

That made me feel more relaxed. I added some more water. It felt like a perfect amount but when I gathered the flour, I realized I still needed more. I added a tiny bit more again and again until it came all together.

"Great job," Dadi said. "Now we have to make the bowl clean."

"What?"

"We have to gather up the dough so well that no one can tell that the bowl was used." She showed me what to do and I worked until the dough was shiny and soft and the inside of the bowl looked clean.

Then we divided it into small balls and rolled each one out flat. Dadi showed me how to cook the roti in a skillet on the stove, first on one side and then on the other, like a pancake.

"Now I'll do the next step," she said.

Dadi placed a roti directly into the flame and it puffed up like a balloon.

"Can I try puffing the next one?" I asked.

She shook her head. "That's too dangerous. But you could spread ghee on it."

I love spreading ghee. It's like buttering toast.

At dinner, Dadi said, "Nina helped me make our food tonight."

"The okra is perfect," Dad said. "Not mushy or sticky."

"And the roti is soft," Mom said.

"I like cooking," I said. "After Dadi leaves can I help you both cook?"

"I'd love that," Mom said.

"You and Kavita already help me make pizza," Dad said. "Maybe you can do more, and I can nap."

Montu and Kavita giggled.

"If you nap, who will put the pizza in the oven?" I asked.

"OK, you can wake me up when it is time to cook it. Until then I can rest."

As I ate a piece of soft roti filled with okra, I thought of how much I was going to miss Dadi and Montu. I started to feel unhappy. By the time I finished chewing my food I had a hard time swallowing it because I was miserable.

Mis-er-a-ble means when you don't feel good and happy.

But I had had a great day with Dadi and Montu. Maybe I was experiencing pain before a fall because I was thinking about their leaving. And that is why even though they were here, I was already missing them.

## CHAPTER THIRTEEN

When Dadi and Montu first arrived, six weeks seemed like a long, long time. Now they were ready to leave, and I felt like they had just gotten here.

Maybe Kavita was right. For the past few weeks, we had been a new family—bigger and different. It was fun to play games with six people rather than just four. I loved cooking, learning Hindi, and trying to meditate with Dadi. When Kavita and I returned from school, Montu was always waiting for us.

Sure, I had given up my room, but that was okay. There

were only a few times I had wanted to be by myself. Now I was used to sharing with Kavita, and I even liked some things about that. Sometimes after we turned out the light, we whispered to each other. We could never do that if we were in separate rooms. I wondered how it would feel to move back to my own bed.

"I wish you lived in Mumbai," Montu said at our last breakfast together. He was having a slice of leftover American pizza—of course, with sugar sprinkled on top.

"If we lived in Mumbai," Kavita said, "I would visit you every weekend."

"Wouldn't it be fun if we could get together whenever we wanted?" I asked.

"No visits." Montu shook his head. "If you lived in Mumbai, we would live together."

I was confused. "Why?"

"Because we are a family. You would live with Dada and Dadi, just like my parents and I do."

"We would?" I looked at Dad as he poured out his tea.

"Montu is right," he said. "I lived with my cousins when I was a kid. It was the best time."

I couldn't believe it. "Mom, did you too?"

"Yes," she said. "There were eight of us. We had fun climbing trees and eating mangoes when we were supposed to be studying."

"You did?" I never knew Mom was that naughty.

"What would we do if we lived together?" Kavita asked.

"We would have fun no matter what we did," Montu said.

*"Fun, fun, that's all we would have, if we lived together. Giggle, giggle, that's all we would do, if we lived together!"* Kavita sang.

I tried to picture what it would be like. Sometimes, even my imagination can't imagine everything I would like to. Right now, my brain was blank. Then I thought if I lived in India, maybe I wouldn't even like American pizza. Maybe I would want sweet pizza.

My face must have scrunched up at the thought, because Kavita asked, "Why are you making a sour face?"

"Sour face?" I asked. "I was thinking of something sweet."

"Oh, like a doughnut?" Kavita asked, "Mom, could we stop for a doughnut on the way to the airport? Please?"

"Sure," Mom said.

I finally got the chance to answer Kavita. "I was thinking about something that is not supposed to be sweet, but it is sweet."

Montu pointed at the sugar bowl. "You mean the way I like my pizza with sugar?"

"That's exactly what I was thinking."

We all laughed.

Around eleven we loaded up the van and drove to the airport. We stopped for doughnuts, and I had my usual, blueberry. Dadi had the same.

All too soon we were at the airport. Before Dadi and Montu went through security, Dadi gave me a goodbye hug and said, "Try to do some meditation when your mind is a jumble of ideas. It will help."

All I could do was nod as I tried to hold back my tears.

Dadi wiped my cheeks. "Don't forget to laugh, my partner."

I saw Dad and Mom sniffling too. Kavita and Montu were the only two who did not cry.

"Montu, I think I'll move to India and live with you one day," Kavita said.

"Really?" I asked. "Won't you miss Mom, Dad, and me?"

"We'll all move there. Right, Dad?" Kavita asked.

Dad kind of nodded. It wasn't an up-and-down nod, but round like Montu's.

Kavita hadn't learned the Montu-nod, but Dad certainly had. Then I wondered how he was able to do it without practicing. I made an in-my-head list.

✱ Since Dad grew up in India, he might have known how to nod that way all along.

✱ But why hadn't I ever seen him do it?

✱ He might have forgotten it once he came to the United States.

* And then after seeing Montu do it, he might have remembered.

* Maybe the Montu-nod is like riding a bicycle or flying a kite. Once you know how to do it, you can never really unknow it. Even if you don't do it very often.

* That could be why Dad was so good at it.

*✻✻*

I fell asleep on the drive home. That was perfect, because otherwise it would have been a long, sad ride.

When we returned home it felt like the four of us were not enough to fill our house. We had gotten used to six people living together, and now two of them were gone.

"We are missing one-third of the family," I said. "It feels strange."

"What does 'one-third' mean?" Kavita asked.

I took six oranges out of the refrigerator. "Just think, the six of us are like six oranges."

"Why do we have to be oranges?" she asked. "Can't we be strawberries? I like them better."

"OK, think of these oranges as strawberries then."

Kavita put her palms over her eyes. "Now I have to imagine the oranges are strawberries?"

"Do you want me to explain, Kavita?" I asked. "Then you have to be quiet."

"Accha." She put her hands down. "Six oranges are like six of us."

I made three piles, each with two oranges. "How many piles are there?"

"Three."

"If we remove one pile of two—which is like Dadi and Montu leaving—then we would be taking one pile out of three away. That is one-third."

"The orange family is separated like our family. These four look sad." She picked up an orange. "I'll eat this one."

"Do you want to move back to your room?" Mom asked me. "I can help you."

"Nina, stay with me," Kavita said. "Just for a few more days. Please?"

"Mom, I think I'll move back after school ends."

Kavita counted on her fingers. "That is almost five days!"

"Nina and Kavita," Mom said, "Dad and I are so proud of you. You were very thoughtful and kind with Dadi and Montu. Nina, you gave up your room, and Kavita, you shared yours with your sister without complaining."

"On top of that you made them both feel not only welcomed but like part of our life," Dad added.

Maybe spending time and having fun with Dadi and Montu made them feel like they were important and special to all of us. They were happy about it. I guess maybe I didn't need to be the perfect hostess all the time.

✱✱✱

When we were getting ready for bed that night, Kavita said, "I wish Dadi and Montu could visit every year."

"Maybe they will," I said. "I think we were good hostesses, so they should want to come back."

Kavita seemed to be thinking about that while we brushed our teeth.

Before we got in bed, I said, "I made a list in Sakhi before they came about how to be a perfect hostess. Maybe we weren't perfect, but we did our best."

Kavita tugged at my sleeve. "Could you read me the list?"

We sat on her bed. I opened Sakhi and read aloud the mature perfect hostess list.

* She is always kind.
* She makes her guests feel welcome.
* She makes sure they're comfortable.
* She is patient when she teaches them something they don't know.
* She doesn't fight with them.

"I think you're right, Nina," Kavita said when I'd finished. "We were kind and made that welcome sign."

I pointed to the list. "We made sure they were comfortable and showed them how everything works, like the shower."

Kavita nodded.

"That was a perfect Montu-nod," I said. "I guess we learned from them, and they learned from us. They were also good guests."

"Montu and I argued and giggled but we never fought."

"Sometimes I was annoyed with him." I closed Sakhi. "It was nice that we had to go to school. I think if we had spent all day, every day with Montu for six weeks, it might have been difficult."

"It might have been impossible to keep giggling all day, every day for six weeks," she said. And giggled.

Mom and Dad came in. "Good night!"

"Good night," we both said and got under the covers.

Mom turned off the light.

Kavita whispered, "I like that you're here, Ninai."

I hugged Kavita. "Me too."

When we walked to school on Monday, Jay said, "I bet you miss Montu and Dadi."

"We do," Kavita said. "But when we move to India, we're going to live with them."

"You're moving?" Jay's green eyes filled with surprise. "To India?"

"That's news to me," I said.

Kavita sang, *"Let us move to India, when we move. And once we do, let us sing with our Montu."*

"You're the only one who sings," I pointed out.

"I was teaching Montu before he left. I just needed a little more time." Kavita turned to Jay. "Do you want to learn?"

"I think Montu is a better student than me. You should teach him."

"Accha," she said and ran to the playground.

Jay and I had a little time before the bell rang, so we watched Kavita and her friends play. "Kavita seems to be excited about India," he said. "Would you like to move there?"

I have only visited India once. I was six, and I remember being careful about not eating anything that was not cooked, meeting too many relatives, and playing with Montu and Kavita in a park that had a big structure shaped like a shoe.

They were nice memories, but one thing was for sure. If we moved to India, I would miss my life here.

I made an in-my-head list of things I would miss.

* My friends, especially Jay, Megan, and Priya
* My school and Ms. Lapin
* Meera Masi and my dance class
* Spring flowers that don't grow in India
* Snow and colorful fall leaves

Jay poked me gently. "Nina."

"I don't want to move to India. I'd miss American pizza."

Jay looked puzzled. "American pizza?"

"Montu thinks our pizza sauce is too sour, so he put

sugar on his," I said. "Jay, before Dadi and Montu came I wanted to be a perfect hostess. I even wrote that in my—" I clamped my mouth shut before more words came out.

"You made a list about being a perfect hostess?" he guessed. "In Sakhi?"

"Yes, I did," I confessed.

Con-fess means to admit something that you might have been keeping a secret.

He shook his head. "You think too much, and you always want to do things the right way."

"Thanks for letting me know that, Jay." Of course, I was being sarcastic, and he knew it.

He pointed to the door, and we began walking just as the bell rang.

Sometimes, Jay and I understand each other without talking, the way Dadi and Montu do. Like right now. When he motioned toward the door, I knew it was time to go in.

Even though I didn't like what Jay had said, I wondered if he was right. I mean, do I think too much about how to do things a certain way—like being a perfect hostess?

I made an in-my-head list of why being a perfect hostess was not a good idea.

* Being a perfect hostess would be too much work.

* Perfection would definitely be too much work to keep up for six weeks, day and night.

* When I tried to be the best all the time, I felt stressed out.

* Stressed-out people can't be perfect hosts or hostesses.

* Then the guest would feel the tension too and be unhappy.

* A hostess needs to be flexible and adjust to her guests' needs.

I remembered all the fun our family had when we went to Olbrich Gardens and to Wisconsin Dells, and when we cooked pizzas. How Dadi and I laughed when she ate a piece of cheese with wax. How my teacher and classmates enjoyed Montu's visit. Then there was Montu's bhangra dances, his and Kavita's giggles, his Montu-nod. I was going to miss all that.

Sitting in the classroom, I realized that I had the most fun when I was relaxed and not trying to be perfect. Maybe being a perfect hostess was not as important as being a kind, relaxed, and attentive hostess.

At-ten-tive means being alert to someone else's need. That way you can be helpful and kind.

Maybe it is not good to try to be a perfect anything.